CODENAME **QUICKSILVER**

Killchase

Look out for the other
CODENAME **QUICKSILVER** books

CODENAME
QUICKSILVER

Killchase

Allan Jones

Orion
Children's Books

With special thanks to Rob Rudderham.

First published in Great Britain in 2013
by Orion Children's Books
a division of the Orion Publishing Group Ltd
Orion House
5 Upper St Martin's Lane
London WC2H 9EA
An Hachette UK company

1 3 5 7 9 10 8 6 4 2

ISBN 978 1 4440 0548 6

Printed in Great Britain by Clays Ltd, St Ives plc

For James Noble

CHAPTER **ONE**

TIME LEFT BEFORE DETONATION: 00:01:23

Zak Archer was finding it difficult to hold the little torch steady between his teeth while he worked on the bomb. The room was in darkness, apart from the small wavering pool of white light, and he needed both hands free to very gently remove the last screw from the casing and lift the curved metal hatch in order to reveal the tangle of wires within.

He tried desperately to remember everything he had been taught in Project 17's Explosive Ordnance

Disposal classes.

This was one time when his special abilities were useless to him. Being able to run like the wind wasn't going to help him in this situation. What was needed here was focus and caution and pinpoint accuracy.

One careless moment, one jittery move, and it would all be over.

The bomb was packed inside a plastic box. Zak had already checked for booby-trap wires on the lid and for the telltale signs that the bomb was radio-controlled. If the trigger was a mobile phone, the device could go off in his face at any moment.

His hands shook and his head throbbed. His body prickled uncomfortably and his heart was pounding so loudly that it felt as if he had a drum under his ribcage.

Cautiously, he removed the hatch from the casing and checked for sensors.

There was a trembler attached to the inside of the casing. If he'd tried to move the bomb, the trembler would have set it off.

His hair was hanging damply in his eyes and he had to keep blinking to clear his vision of stinging sweat.

He glanced at the digital countdown. 00:01:02.

If this were a movie, he'd be choosing between the

red and the green wires. Which to cut? *Red? No! Green?*
No ... wait ...

Except that all the wires in the bomb were yellow.

Using the tip of his tongue, Zak angled the torch beam
to one side.

Gotcha!

He could see the battery pack in its TPU casing: the
heart and brain of the bomb.

He lifted a shaking hand and slid his fingers in through
the yellow wires.

The trembler wire quivered.

Stop.

Breathe. Calm down. Forget the cramp growing in
your legs. Forget the countdown.

His hand slid deeper into the device, brushing past
the wires.

He stopped breathing. The blood surged through his
head, making it hard to concentrate.

His fingertips reached the micro-plug in the battery.

He took it between the sides of his index and
forefinger and gently eased it out.

It came loose and fell away.

The digital display stopped at 00:00:27.

Zak rocked back on his heels and let out a long whoop
of breath.

Lights flickered on.

"Well done, Quicksilver."

It was Colonel Hunter's voice, coming over an intercom.

Zak spat the torch into his palm and stood up. His legs were still shaking, but all the worry and uncertainty had already drained away.

He gave a relieved smile as he gazed across the room to the mirror that almost filled one wall. In the reflection, he could see the various items of training and fitness equipment that surrounded him.

There was a room behind the mirror, and in that room he knew there were a group of people who had been watching him work on the bomb.

"How did I do?" he called.

"You'll get your official assessment in due course," came the Colonel's disembodied voice. "But you haven't finished yet."

The door opened and Dr Jackson entered, followed by a few other white-coats. One of them scuttled over to the bomb, peered into it and scribbled some notes on a clipboard.

"Good morning, Quicksilver," said Dr Jackson, blinking at Zak from behind his thick horn-rimmed glasses. He gestured across the room. "The treadmill, if you don't mind."

Zak didn't mind at all. Trying to defuse a dummy bomb in front of a whole lot of hidden observers had been nerve-wracking, but running a few kilometres on a treadmill would be fun. It would also help release the energy that he'd built up over the past few hours while he'd been reading and re-reading his bomb disposal notes.

A couple of the white-coats attached sticky monitor pads to Zak's chest, back and temples and fed thin wires into various electronic devices set up by the treadmill.

"We'll start easy, then see how it goes," said Dr Jackson as Zak climbed onto the treadmill.

"Fine with me." Zak glanced again at the long mirror. He didn't know exactly who was behind there, apart from Colonel Hunter, but he was aware that they were VIPs and he was determined to give them a good show.

Dr Jackson set the speed of the treadmill and the black conveyer belt began to move. Zak jogged along. The pace was way too easy. He was never going to burn off any energy at this rate.

Dr Jackson increased the speed slightly. Zak ran along, putting his hands into his pockets and yawning. He saw one or two of the white-coats grinning.

"Are we starting the test soon?" Zak asked with a wry smile.

Dr Jackson pressed some buttons and the treadmill began to move faster.

"Subject is now running at ten kilometres an hour," Dr Jackson said, speaking to the watchers behind the window. "I have him on an incline of twelve per cent. His heart rate is at the level one would expect from this degree of exertion. All stress monitors are showing reactions that fall within usual parameters."

"Boring!" Zak said with a grin. "Crank it up a bit more, doc, I'm falling asleep here!" He was really beginning to enjoy himself. "Kidding!" he added. He didn't want Colonel Hunter to think he was getting big-headed.

Dr Jackson punched a few more buttons. The belt was whipping away beneath Zak's feet now. His hands were out of his pockets, the lazy grin gone from his face as his arms pumped at his sides.

"Subject now running at twenty kilometres per hour," Dr Jackson said, his eyes on the treadmill's display screen. "Heart rate rising."

Zak ran, staring straight ahead, ignoring everything around him. He was close to his special place. He was nearly in the zone – that point where the gears in his head and body seemed to mesh and running became effortless.

Zak was so focused on his running he was only

vaguely aware of Dr Jackson's voice now. "This is where it starts to get interesting," Dr Jackson was saying. "Watch your monitors, ladies and gentlemen. You will see that the heart rate has settled to a lower level than previously, and you will also see how the imbalance in the subject's adrenal gland is showing as increased activity in the hypothalamus. But note also that the increase in adrenaline is not causing the normal rise in blood pressure, nor the expected vascular constriction."

Dr Jackson tapped the buttons again and the belt was really flying. Zak was in the zone, sprinting at full speed, breathing steadily. His legs were working like pistons, his arms swinging smoothly at his sides as he breathed calmly in and out. He felt tireless and elated. He felt as if he could carry on doing this for the rest of the day.

"Subject is running at forty kilometres per hour," said Dr Jackson. "And this is where things really begin to get strange."

Zak grinned.

Effortlessly in the zone.

On the other side of the long two-way mirror, a row of chairs faced into the large training room where Zak was being put through his paces. Clamped to the arm of each chair was a tablet computer displaying the data being produced by Dr Jackson's diagnostic devices.

"Dealing with the bomb proves the boy is capable of the intelligent and skilled application of learned techniques," said a severe-looking but attractive woman in her forties. She looked at Colonel Hunter. "But that's not what we're here for, is it?" She was Colonel Pearce, head of the MI5 department that worked out of Citadel, one of the four subterranean secret services bases that existed under London: Fortress, Rampart, Bastion and Citadel.

"Not entirely," replied Colonel Hunter. "I thought it would be useful for you to see that he's capable of using his brain, as well as being gifted in other ways."

"I can see what you mean," said an elderly man with white hair and a neat beard. Major Connolly, head of Rampart, leaned forwards, staring through the mirror. "He's a remarkable child."

Lieutenant Colonel McDermott, head of Bastion, was a short, stocky man with a face like a bulldog. "Do you have any more like him hidden away, Colonel?" he growled.

Colonel Hunter gave a quiet smile. "Quicksilver is a one-off, as far as we know," he said. "Dr Jackson tells us his abilities come from a glandular imbalance. Normally, the amount of adrenaline his body releases would be dangerous, but somehow he absorbs it and uses it to his advantage. Dr Jackson says he's never seen anything like it before."

"I can believe that," said Isadora Reed, an American woman wearing a smart and expensive business suit. "He's quite the athlete." Her face was tanned and her voice had the sharp tone of someone used to being obeyed. "But does he have any other tricks up his sleeve, Peter?"

"Possibly," said the Colonel. "That's something Dr Jackson is trying to find out."

"For what length of time can the boy run at forty kilometres per hour?" asked Lieutenant Colonel McDermott.

"I don't believe he's been tested to his limit," said Colonel Hunter. "We're moving forwards carefully with him. The last thing we want to do is to burn him out or cause him some permanent injury."

"No," said the American woman. "I can see how you'd want to preserve such a precious asset, Peter." She leaned back, crossing her legs, her eyes narrowing as she watched Zak running in the other room. "He's an extraordinary piece of equipment. Would you consider loaning him out? There are some tests we could do back in Washington that would certainly reveal his potential."

"Not at the moment," Mr Mallin, Personal Private Secretary to the Home Secretary, broke in. He was the youngest man in the room, somewhere in his thirties, tall and pale and wearing a pinstriped suit. He gave Isadora Reed a thin smile. "We'd like to know a lot more about him before we allow the FBI to get their hands on him."

Isadora Reed laughed. "You can't blame a girl for trying, John," she said casually. She looked at Colonel Hunter. "The Project 17 report on Operation Burning Sky says he showed impressive strength at one point. But it was a little vague on the details. What happened, Peter?"

"The Burning Sky device had been fixed to a brick wall with six ten-millimetre coach bolts," Colonel Hunter explained. "A fully grown man would have needed a crowbar and a lot of muscle to get it loose. From his report, it seems that Quicksilver pulled it off the wall with his bare hands in about fifteen seconds."

"Impressive," said Colonel Pearce. "And have you replicated this feat of strength, to see if he can repeat it at will?"

"Not yet," said the Colonel. "Quicksilver cut his hands quite badly when he did it, and we've been waiting for his injuries to heal completely."

Isadora Reed tapped her nails on the arm of her chair, watching Zak closely. "You seem to have a real super-agent here, Peter," she said quietly. "Are we going to see some tests of his strength today?"

"That's the plan," replied Colonel Hunter. He pressed a button on his computer. "Dr Jackson? Move it along, please." He nodded towards the treadmill, where Zak was still sprinting. "Watch closely," he said, leaning back. "This could be very interesting."

"Hey! I was enjoying that!" Zak said as Dr Jackson tapped out a command on the treadmill console and the belt began to slow down. "I could have carried on all day."

"I think that's probably a good reason to stop," said Dr Jackson. "I'd like to test you on some other equipment now, Quicksilver."

"Fine," said Zak, jumping off the belt. "Whatever you say."

Zak's confidence had come a long way since Colonel Hunter had first suggested he might have the ability to become a Project 17 agent. Several months and a whole lot of physical and academic training later, Zak was beginning to feel as if he could handle anything the Colonel threw at him. Okay, so he'd sweated over that bomb, but he'd defused it safely with almost half a minute to spare.

Dr Jackson led him over to one of the weight machines, a heavy-duty piece of equipment with a leather seat and a lot of tubular steel attachments. Zak's fellow agent, Jackhammer, spent a lot of time on this machine, pumping his muscles till you could almost have painted him green and called him the Hulk. Zak wasn't as muscular as Jackhammer, but he was looking forward to testing himself on this particular piece of equipment.

Ripping the Burning Sky device off the wall had been totally amazing. He still couldn't quite believe he'd done it. All that strength – out of nowhere! If Colonel Hunter hadn't insisted he take time to recover, he'd already have given some of these machines a good workout, just to prove to himself it hadn't been a one-off.

"This machine comes with two levels of pulleys, pec fly, leg extension and curl," Dr Jackson said, talking to the watchers again. "It's capable of working all the major muscle groups and includes a weight stack that can generate over fifty kilos of resistance in certain exercises." He looked at Zak. "We'll start you off easy," he said. "Don't try to go beyond your natural limits."

Zak climbed onto the seat. "What would you like me to do first?" he asked, settling down.

"I think we'll start with the upper body," said Dr Jackson as the other white-coats gathered around.

"Okay, ready or not, here I go." Zak reached up and grabbed the rubber handles that were suspended from the steel frame above his head.

The running thing came so naturally to him that it didn't seem all that special – but summoning super-strength at will, that would really be something to feel proud of. He hoped he could do it. He didn't want to fail in front of Colonel Hunter and the others behind the mirror.

"Okay, Quicksilver, I think that will do for today," said Dr Jackson.

Zak had no idea how much time had passed. He felt as if he'd been on that machine for hours.

Super-strength? Super-loser, more like.

The workout had been a total disaster.

Well, no, not a total disaster, but he could tell Dr Jackson was disappointed in his performance. As he'd come to the limit of his capabilities in each different exercise, he'd heard Dr Jackson say something like, "Thank you, Quicksilver, that was good for a boy of

your age. Shall we move on?"

In other words, he was doing fine, but there was nothing spectacular happening: no great surge of strength like he'd felt when he'd pulled the Burning Sky device off the wall; no rush of power; no moment when he felt that *thing* in his head that meant he was in the zone.

Colonel Hunter's voice came over the intercom. "Go and take a shower, Quicksilver," he said. "Report to my office in thirty minutes."

Exhausted and deflated, Zak wandered to the showers. He let the hot water beat into his face. He'd failed. The strength thing must have been a one-off fluke. He wasn't so very special after all.

He was just some freak who could run fast.

Big deal.

CHAPTER **TWO**

"Can I try again?" Zak asked the Colonel the moment he entered his office. "I can do better than that, I know I can."

Colonel Hunter and Dr Jackson were at a side table, leaning over a computer with a screen full of graphs and charts.

"Take a seat, Quicksilver," said the Colonel, without looking around.

Zak sat, watching the two men as they spoke in low voices. Every so often Dr Jackson clicked the mouse to change the screen.

Zak had the definite feeling they were discussing his pathetic performance in the training room. No, 'pathetic' was too harsh – *ordinary* was probably a better word for it.

"I think I just had a bad day," Zak said uneasily. "Maybe tomorrow . . ." His voice trailed off. He felt empty and disappointed.

"Thank you, doctor," said Colonel Hunter, straightening up. "I'd like your full report on my desk by seventeen hundred hours today."

"It'll be there," said Dr Jackson. He smiled reassuringly at Zak. "You gave us a lot of very useful data today, agent," he said. "Don't be too hard on yourself."

Easy for you to say!

Dr Jackson left the office and Colonel Hunter sat down behind his desk. "Dr Jackson is right," said the Colonel. "You shouldn't expect too much of yourself." He raised an eyebrow. "We don't need you to be a superhero, Quicksilver."

Zak sighed, not feeling much better. "I was really hoping to develop X-ray vision and the power of flight," he joked in a flat voice.

A smile twitched the corner of Colonel Hunter's mouth. "All in good time," he replied. "For the moment, be content that the people who saw you today went away very impressed."

"Who were they?" Zak asked.

"The heads of the other three special ops departments in the Underground," Colonel Hunter replied. The Underground was the collective name of the four hidden MI5 divisions. "A representative of the Home Secretary, and a guest from the FBI."

"The FBI?" repeated Zak, perking up. "From America?"

"Indeed," said the Colonel. "All kinds of people are interested in you, Quicksilver."

"Wow," said Zak. "I wish I'd done better."

Colonel Hunter ignored Zak's comment. "Have your hands fully recovered?" he asked.

Zak showed his palms to the Colonel. The cuts and abrasions had healed well. There weren't even any scars. "When superheroes rip metal apart with their bare hands in the movies, they don't cut themselves to pieces," said Zak. "Why is that?"

"Because it isn't real," replied the Colonel. "Don't start confusing fact with science fiction, Quicksilver. You have unique abilities. And in time, I'm sure you'll discover a lot more about them."

"But not today," said Zak.

"No, not today." Colonel Hunter smiled. "But I didn't ask you here to discuss your performance," he continued. "You're here because I received a phone call this morning that I think will be of interest to you."

Zak frowned at him. A phone call? Who would be calling him here? Who outside Fortress even knew Project 17 existed, far less had its phone number?

"When you left the children's home, we gave the local council a contact number for you," Colonel Hunter explained. "It was one of your old residential care workers who got in touch."

"Oh." That was unexpected. Since leaving the children's home, Zak had had virtually no contact with the people in Robert Wyatt House. At first he had been too busy – overwhelmed by the workload that was generated by his new life. And it wasn't as if he could stroll over there and tell them the truth about what he was doing anyway. Then, as weeks stretched into months, he began to lose any desire to return. Fortress was his home now, and his fellow Project 17 agents were his friends and family. He'd moved on.

"They have received a package addressed to you," said the Colonel. "Normally, I'd have asked them to forward it to the postbox we use for such things, but I thought perhaps in this case you'd like to go and pick it up in person. It would give you the chance to see some of your old friends – I know you haven't had much time to do that since you've been with Project 17."

"Oh. Yes. That would be great, thanks." Zak was taken aback by the offer. He really had no idea how he'd feel about returning to the children's home all these months later.

"You're due some downtime, I believe," said the Colonel. "You can go and pick up the package this afternoon, if you wish."

Zak nodded.

"Dismissed," said the Colonel.

Zak got up to leave.

"Stonewall Protocols, Quicksilver," said the Colonel, as he headed for the door.

"Of course," said Zak.

Stonewall Protocols: there is no such organization as Project 17. There is no such place as Fortress.

Colonel Hunter?

Never heard of him.

Zak sat on a bench in Jubilee Gardens, gazing out over the River Thames. To his left, the huge hoop of the London Eye was revolving slowly. Across the river the skyline of London was a confusion of glass and steel towers and ancient church spires.

The package was lying unopened on his lap. It was a padded white envelope, measuring about fifteen by twenty centimetres and probably three centimetres thick.

It was addressed to:

Zachary Archer,
c/o Robert Wyatt House,
Lychgate St,
LONDON SE1

Zak was thinking about his brief visit to the children's home. It had been a weird experience, like stepping back into someone else's life. The place seemed to have shrunk in his absence. Had he lived here for four years? *Really?* He wasn't that kid any more. Not by a long way.

Shrugging off his thoughts, he picked up the envelope and ripped the end open. Inside were a small mobile phone and a photograph. He shook them into his hand.

A sensation like an electric shock burned through him as he stared down at the photograph.

It was a snapshot of a family. A man and woman smiled into the camera while a boy of about eight stood close by. The woman had a baby in her arms.

Zak knew this photo. He had seen it once before – in Colonel Hunter's office in Fortress.

It was a photo of his mother and father and his older brother, Jason.

And the baby? The baby was ten days old.

The baby was Zak.

The photograph had been taken only a few weeks before his parents had been killed in a plane crash. Colonel Hunter's words drilled into his brain as he gazed at the photo, hardly able to breathe.

"Your mother was a respected MI5 field agent with ten years' experience. She had been working on a special case for the previous eighteen months, trying to pin down the identity of a terrorist leader who went by the name Reaperman."

Zak had known for several months some of the details of how his parents had died, but it was only recently that Colonel Hunter had told him the name of the terrorist thought to be responsible for their deaths. A name with an unpleasant ring to it: Reaperman.

He was the mastermind behind a major terrorist organization. No one knew what he looked like. No one knew how to find him. It was said that he slept in a different bed in a different house every night; that he moved smoothly from country to country like a malicious ghost.

Any agent who had come close to learning his secrets had disappeared or been found dead. Reaperman had a terrible reputation. If you got in his way he wouldn't only kill *you*, he would kill your whole family. He would burn your house to the ground; he would utterly destroy you and everyone who ever meant anything to you.

When the plane carrying Janet and John Trent had been brought down in Canada, MI5 had initiated its highest security protocols to protect their two boys.

"Your brother was adopted by a family named Wyndham," Colonel Hunter had told Zak. "At the age of eighteen, he was recruited by MI5 and given the codename Slingshot. I am not in a position to give you any information concerning his whereabouts."

"But he's alive?" Zak had asked eagerly.

"He is alive," the Colonel had replied. "And when the time is right, and it is safe to do so, I'll tell you more. But for now, you must be patient, Quicksilver."

But Jason Wyndham was alive. Slingshot was alive.

At least Zak had been given the hope that one day he might meet Jason.

He snapped back into the present. His hands shaking, he turned the photograph over. Something had been scribbled on the back.

Go somewhere you can't be overheard, then activate the phone. I'll call you.

Zak's voice was a whisper. "Jason?"

CHAPTER **THREE**

"No." A young man's voice came down the phone. "I'm not your brother, Zak. My name is Gabriel."

Zak's heart sank. The disappointment hit him like a punch in the stomach.

"Where are you, Zak? Are you alone?" came the young man's voice. He sounded urgent and deadly serious.

"Who are you?" Zak said. "What's all this about?"

"*Are you alone?*" insisted the voice.

"Yes."

"Are you in Fortress?"

This guy knew about Fortress? "No," Zak snapped.

"Tell me what this is all about. Why did you send me that picture?"

"To try and convince you that what I'm about to tell you is true," said Gabriel. "I'm an MI5 agent. I was teamed with your brother for a while just after he'd joined the Service."

Zak listened, startled and fascinated, not knowing whether to believe him.

"I've been in deep cover for two and a half years now," Gabriel continued. "On a top-secret mission in Europe."

"Is Jason on the same mission?" asked Zak.

"I'm sorry, Zak, but I can't tell you," said Gabriel. "It's vital that his cover isn't compromised. It's the same for all of us. A security breach could cost us our lives."

So, Jason was doing something so important that not even a whisper or a hint could be let out. Zak's mind reeled.

"I've found something out," said Gabriel. "Something really bad."

Zak gulped. "About Jason?" he asked.

"No." There was a pause. "I'm convinced there's a mole in an important position in British Intelligence. You know what a mole is, don't you?"

"A traitor," said Zak. "Someone who feeds classified information to our enemies."

"That's right," said Gabriel. "Someone high up in the chain of command in MI5 is handing over our secrets to an international terrorist organization."

"Who?" demanded Zak. He wasn't just going to take Gabriel's word that someone in a position of authority had turned traitor.

"I don't know," Gabriel replied. "But it compromises the safety of the entire country. You get that, don't you? If a terrorist organization has information about our secret services, they'd know how to bypass all our security systems. They'd be able to run rings around us. They could use our own codes to send us off on a wild-goose chase while they planted bombs that could kill hundreds of people. And that might be only the start." Zak could hear the urgency in Gabriel's voice. "I've come up with a way to flush the mole out," he continued. "But I'm going to need help. I'm going to need *you*, Zak."

For a few moments, Zak was too surprised to respond. He couldn't figure it out. Who was Gabriel? What did he really want? Why did he need Zak? The whole thing was just too weird.

"Can I rely on you?" asked the voice. "Will you help me?"

Alarm bells began to ring. This was all wrong.

"I'll tell you what I'm going to do," Zak said. "I'm going

to find out what Colonel Hunter thinks of all this."

"No!" Gabriel's response was like a whipcrack. "You can't do that. You *cannot* go to Hunter with this. Don't you get it, Zak? I'm certain the mole is high up in British Intelligence – very high up – in a position of enormous authority. For all I know, it may be Hunter himself."

"That's crazy," said Zak, becoming annoyed now. "Anyone who thinks Colonel Hunter is a traitor must be totally mental."

"You could be right," said Gabriel. "But what if the mole is one of the other department heads?" His voice became even more urgent. "What if it's McDermott in Bastion, or Pearce in Citadel or Connolly in Rampart? What if it's someone from the office of MI5's Director General? It could be someone who Colonel Hunter reports to. Someone who works with the Home Secretary." Gabriel's voice sounded more calm now. "Listen to me, Zak. This is the most important decision you will ever have to make. Either you trust me and help your country – or you go to Hunter and risk the mole being alerted. One or the other. It's as simple as that."

"No, it's even *simpler* than that," said Zak, pushing the photograph back into the envelope and standing up. "I'm not falling for it, okay? I'm not playing." Anger bubbled up in him. "You must think I'm a total idiot."

Gabriel was perfectly controlled. "I thought you might need more convincing," he said. "You've come a long way since Ballerina made a fool of you."

Zak froze. Gabriel knew about Ballerina? She was a Project 17 agent who had been going to betray her country, and who had almost tricked Zak into helping her. Whoever this guy was, he definitely had access to some pretty secure information. Was that a good or a bad sign?

"How do you know about Ballerina?" Zak asked cautiously.

"I'm not going to reveal my methods," said Gabriel. "I have ways of reading secure files remotely. That includes Project 17 files."

"Are you some kind of hacker?" Zak asked. All Project 17 files were meant to be fireproof. Gabriel must have some pretty sophisticated software if he could get through the firewalls that Bug had installed in the system.

"I can get into the files," Gabriel replied. "That's all you need to know." There was a brief pause. "Look, I have a way to convince you that I'm genuine, that I'm on the side of the angels."

"I'm listening," Zak said, still intending to take this straight to Colonel Hunter.

"I'm going to give you a code," said Gabriel. "It will allow you access to your brother's personal file. There's information in there that I think will interest you."

Colonel Hunter had been unwilling to tell Zak much about his brother. The thought that he could read the file for himself was tempting. But the idea that a man he knew nothing about could just hack into Project 17's computers made him very uneasy.

"Tell you what," he snapped. "Get Jason to give me a call, and I'll think about it." He turned and walked across the lawns of Jubilee Gardens, heading towards Waterloo Bridge, intending to get back to Fortress as quickly as possible and tell Colonel Hunter this whole incredible story.

"Jason can't do that, Zak," said Gabriel. "I told you, he can't risk breaking cover. He could be killed if the people he's watching find out who he really is."

"Why should I trust you?" said Zak. "Forget it."

"Listen to me!" Gabriel's voice was persuasive. "The code is AVIDON1619. Go to Fortress and check it out. That's all I'm asking, Zak. Check that the code works and take a look at your brother's file. The rest is up to you. Either you believe what I'm telling you and decide to help me – or you go to Hunter and risk the mole disappearing into the long grass."

Zak hesitated. There was no way any of this was true. But what if the code really did work? What if he could open his brother's codeword-locked file and find out what was in there?

Ever since he'd discovered he had a brother, Zak had been desperate to learn more about him. Colonel Hunter had his own reasons for not telling Zak everything – but that didn't stop Zak wanting more.

AVIDON1619.

Would that unlock the secrets Zak was longing to know?

"Okay," Zak said. "I'll think about it. But first you need to explain one thing. Why are you coming to me with this? Why me?"

"You're an expert at free running, aren't you, Zak?" said Gabriel. "I read about it in your file. You can run faster than anyone else, and you can jump further. I need someone with those specific abilities, Zak. I need you."

"You're going to have to tell me more than that," said Zak. He had spent half his life enjoying the thrill of free running; his adrenaline-fuelled speed and agility made him almost impossible to catch once he got going.

"I need to know you're on my side before I tell you anything else," Gabriel replied.

"So now you don't trust *me*?" said Zak.

"We have to find out if we can trust each other," said Gabriel. "Go and look at the file. Then decide."

"Okay," Zak said. "But don't hold your breath."

"That's good, Zak," said Gabriel, sounding relieved. "The phone I sent you is a burner – do you know what that means?"

"It's a prepaid phone that only works for a limited time," said Zak. "Crooks use them because they're difficult to trace."

"Not only crooks," said Gabriel. "Us good guys use them too."

Zak gave a noncommittal grunt.

"Your phone has a seventy-two-hour lifespan," said Gabriel. "Switch it off when we're finished. If you decide you want to help me, leave your Mob at Fortress and go to Victoria train station. You'll be too easy to track if you have your Mob. When you get to the station, turn the phone back on and wait for me to call."

The Mob was a Project 17 issue smartphone. Silvery, oval, as thin as a credit card. Cutting-edge technology.

"Even if I did that, how would you know when to call me?" Zak asked.

"I'll call every thirty minutes," said Gabriel. "Goodbye, Zak. I hope you make the right decision."

The phone went dead.

Zak stared at it for a few moments, then pressed the button to turn it off. He dropped it back into the padded envelope and stuffed it inside his jacket.

He broke into a smooth jog, making for the bridge and the nearest entrance into Fortress. He didn't trust the mysterious man who had called himself Gabriel. Not one bit. But if there was a chance he could learn more about his brother, the MI5 agent with the codename Slingshot, he was going to take that chance – and risk the fallout.

Zak lay sleepless on his bed that night. He was fully clothed. Watching the digital display on his bedside clock. Waiting.

Every now and then he took the photo of the Trent family out of the envelope and stared at it, trying to imagine himself as that baby – trying to capture the feel of his mother's arms around him.

It was hopeless. His parents had been dead for fourteen years. His brother was away on a dangerous mission. He had never known them. He couldn't imagine himself as part of a family. He didn't even know how he *should* feel about them.

The only emotion that burned in him was the desire to know the truth – to find out every detail of their lives.

And the way to find out about Jason was by looking at his file. Zak already knew the best place to do that – Bug's office, the computerized heart of Fortress.

At last, he got up and padded to the door. He was wearing socks. No shoes. He listened, his heart thudding. All was strangely quiet.

He slipped out into the corridor. It was brightly lit as always, but there was no one around. He closed his door silently and padded down the corridor towards Bug's office.

He went into the darkened room and closed the door behind him. The bank of eight plasma screens above Bug's desk glowed with a soft, aquamarine light.

Bug's collection of frogs stared at Zak as he crept to the chair. Frogs gazed down from wall posters. They peered at Zak from the top of every spare surface: beanbag frogs, plastic frogs, wind-up frogs, origami frogs. Bug had an obsession with frogs. Bug was a genius when it came to computers, but he was also a little bit strange . . . in a good way.

Zak settled into Bug's big leather chair and pulled the keyboard onto his knees. He took out his tiny pencil-torch and twisted it to activate its thin white beam. Holding the end of the torch between his teeth to leave both hands free for typing, he opened a browser and found the search history.

He went to the search box. He typed, frowning as he picked out the letters he wanted. He needed to find a page he'd seen Bug working on a while ago. He thought he knew the correct wording to bring it up.

He pressed ENTER. The closest plasma screen flashed into life. A blue page opened.

SECURITY SERVICES – MI5. ALPHA CLEARANCE
FILES. EYES ONLY. NO HARD COPIES.

Yes! That's the one. Excellent.

He rolled the mouse-wheel on the keyboard so that the cursor hit the search box.

Zak typed SLINGSHOT and clicked on ENTER.

The screen flickered and new wording came up.

SEARCH RESULTS.
Searched for Slingshot. Result 1. Search took 0.09
seconds.
MI5 Agent Slingshot.
Real name: JASON TRENT, AKA JASON
WYNDHAM.
Authorization code: ALPHA-LOCKED FILE.
MINISTERIAL CLEARANCE NEEDED.

Zak began to tremble with anticipation. His mouth was dry. He knew what that meant. No one was allowed access to Slingshot's file without the direct approval of the Home Secretary.

Below the wording, there was another box.

Zak clicked on it and began to type.

AVIDON1619

He touched the ENTER key.

The page changed.

Slingshot's file appeared on screen.

Zak took the torch out of his mouth and let out a slow, whistling breath.

Gabriel had been telling the truth – about the access code at least.

He was in his brother's restricted file.

He started to read, his lips moving, the words coming out in a soft whisper.

Following the deaths of Janet and John Trent, it was believed that the lives of their children were in direct jeopardy. Their two sons were taken into the protective custody of MI5's relocation department. To ensure complete anonymity and to give them the best chance of survival, the brothers were separated. (For a better understanding of the need for such swift and drastic action, see file TOW396758433RM/00452, which gives a full account of the retribution paid out by Reaperman on the families of agents who came too close to him.)

Zak shuddered. Colonel Hunter had told him about this. He didn't need to read a list of murders and revenge attacks to know that Reaperman was terminally dangerous to anyone who got in his way.

Swallowing hard, he continued to read aloud.

"Despite being eight years old, Jason Trent was quickly adopted by a naturalized British couple named Wyndham. The father, Stephano Wyndham, is half-Greek on the maternal side and the mother, Kavitha, is of Indian origin. Jason took their surname and was brought up in Guildford, Surrey."

Zak tried to ignore a stab of envy at the pleasant childhood his brother seemed to have enjoyed. Zak had been shuttled from foster home to foster home, never settling anywhere, until he'd finally washed up at Robert Wyatt House at the age of ten.

Jason had always shown an unusual talent with languages, and was already fluent in German,

French and Italian when he became part of the Wyndham household. Living with multilingual parents, Jason soon became adept in Greek and Hindi too, and by the time he reached his early teens he was also able to speak and write Spanish, Portuguese and Russian.

Zak was impressed. He'd never found foreign languages easy, and yet his brother was able to chat away in seven or more different languages. *If I read something about him being able to run super-fast, I'm really going to start disliking him*, Zak thought with the faintest flicker of humour.

By this time, Jason began asking for more information about his birth parents. He knew the Trents had been killed in a plane crash in Canada, and that his mother had worked for the British government, but he wanted more. Though files on Janet Trent were classified as top secret and archived in MI5, it was decided that, after a gap of several years, it would be safe to give Jason some details of Janet and John Trent. He was told that his birth mother had worked for British Intelligence and that she had

been killed on active duty along with his birth
father.

Zak wondered how Jason had taken that piece of
information. What was easier? Never to have known
your parents, or to have lived with them for eight years
and then to find out long after they were dead that they
had a secret life you knew nothing about?

It seems this information inspired Jason to follow
in his mother's footsteps. On moving to secondary
school, Jason began to concentrate more and
more on increasing his skill with languages, both
at school and with private tutors paid for by the
Wyndhams. Knowing that British Intelligence was
always on the lookout for university graduates
with a working knowledge of Arabic, he
specialized in modern standard Arabic and also
in various colloquial varieties of the language,
intending to study those subjects when he went
to university.

Zak tried to picture Jason working away hour after
hour, year after year, at those languages, in the hope
of getting the same job that had killed his mother and

father. Who would do that? And then Zak remembered the hours, days and weeks he had spent in training to become a fully fledged Project 17 agent.

Were he and Jason more alike than he had imagined?

Zak hadn't known about his parents' fate when he had joined Project 17. But learning about it hadn't stopped him, had it? If anything, it had made him more determined to succeed.

Unusually, Jason Wyndham was recruited by MI5 at the age of eighteen, expressly because of his facility with languages. He was put through the usual training protocols and, having passed with top grades in all fields, he was given the codename Slingshot. At this point he was allocated a mission and teamed with an agent who had been recruited at the more usual age of twenty-one. His fellow agent was codenamed Archangel.*

Zak sat back. He was suffering information overload. There was so much to take in.

His mother had been a secret agent. His brother was a secret agent. And now *he* was a secret agent. How weird was that? What was he going to find out next? That his granny and granddad had worked for MI5 too?

There was an asterisk that led to a footnote.

First-year Agent Slingshot was placed with
Archangel because of the slightly older agent's
exemplary record and the eminent family from
which he comes. Archangel is a computer
expert as well as being highly skilled in the
use of explosives. There is no young agent
better suited to overseeing the early career of a
colleague. (See Archangel's file for more details.)

Eminent family? Zak had heard the word *eminent*
before – it meant really special. So, Archangel must be
the son of someone super-trustworthy. Interesting.

Then something clicked in Zak's head.

Jason had been teamed up with someone codenamed
Archangel.

Wasn't there an archangel called Gabriel?

Yes. Definitely. The Archangel Gabriel. And Gabriel
had said he was on the side of the angels. That must have
been a clue. Plus he'd told Zak he'd been partnered with
Jason just after he'd joined MI5. Gabriel and Archangel
had to be the same person. This was beyond interesting.
This changed everything.

Zak turned back to the file and scrolled down to continue reading. He was almost certain that Gabriel could be trusted now. He just needed to read a little more.

He gave a start as the light went on above his head.

He spun around. A figure stood in the doorway.

Busted!

CHAPTER **FOUR**

"What are you doing, Silver?" asked Bug, stepping into the room. The twelve-year-old computer genius was wearing his pyjamas. His hair was ruffled and his eyes were puffy from sleep.

"You scared the life out of me!" Zak exclaimed. "How did you know I was here?"

"I have an alarm system set up in case anyone tries to access my computers," said Bug. "It woke me up. It's quite noisy. I sampled the territorial call of an American bullfrog." He rubbed his eyes. "It's ten decibels louder than a lion's roar, on average," he added. "Not many people know that."

Of course Bug would set an alarm. Zak should have known.

Bug walked over to the chair. The door closed softly behind him. He stared at the plasma screen. His eyes bulged beneath his fringe. His breath came out in a hiss.

"How did you get into that file?" he said, and now there was suspicion in his voice. "How did you hack it?"

"I didn't," Zak replied, watching Bug carefully, wondering what he would do next. "I was given the code."

"These files are totally restricted," said Bug. "Who gave you the code?" His eyes grew even wider. "Who even *had* the code to give you?" He frowned. "It would have to be Control's grade or higher. Did Colonel Hunter give you the code?" A look of confusion came over his face. "No, not Control. That's crazy." It had only taken Bug a split second to realize that Zak must be here without proper authorization. "Who was it?" There was real alarm in Bug's voice now.

Zak looked at Bug, not knowing how much he should tell him.

A moment passed while the two of them stared at one another, then Bug lunged forwards, snatched the keyboard from Zak, and pressed a key that shut down the screen.

"They'll be able to tell that the page was opened," Bug muttered, typing rapidly. "I need to confuse them, make it a lot less obvious which terminal was using the page." He glanced at Zak and shook his head. "You're such an idiot, Zak. You're lucky I found you first. Do you know the penalty for accessing restricted files?"

"Something pretty bad, I'd guess," said Zak, beginning to feeling guilty that he had gone behind Bug's back. "But I had to take the risk."

Bug pressed a final key and let out a relieved breath. "There, that should give them something to think about." He glared at Zak. "Now, tell me what's going on."

Zak's brain was working fast, trying to make sense of what he had learned over the past few hours. It was clear now to him that Gabriel was the MI5 agent codenamed Archangel, which meant that what he'd told Zak about the existence of a mole was probably true. But was that enough for him to withhold information from Colonel Hunter? To go off who-knows-where without telling anyone? Was Gabriel right when he said that *no one* should be trusted?

Zak decided that yes, he was. For the moment, at least.

"Something strange is going on," Zak began, as Bug hovered over him.

"No kidding?" murmured Bug. "Is it something to do

with your brother?"

Zak eyed him for a moment before speaking.

How much to tell Bug? Zak had made up his mind what he was going to do next. He would go to Victoria station as Gabriel had asked. He would switch on the mobile phone and he would wait for the call. And he would do all this without letting Colonel Hunter know.

"An undercover MI5 agent has got in touch with me." Zak paused, wondering how Bug would react. "He needs me to do something important. I have to do it very soon and I have to do it without telling anyone."

"You're sure he's in MI5?" asked Bug. "You're certain this isn't a trick of some kind?"

Zak nodded. "He knows my brother. I'm sure he's telling the truth."

"The truth about what?" asked Bug.

"He asked me not to say," Zak said, unwilling to reveal more than was absolutely necessary. "But if it's true, it's really bad, Bug." He wracked his brains for the right way to put this. "If it is true, I need to go away for a while."

Bug's eyes were wide. "Where?"

Zak shook his head. "I don't know." He couldn't have told Bug even if he'd wanted to. He had no idea where Gabriel's secret mission might lead him.

Bug was very quiet for a few moments, staring down

at the floor, shifting from foot to foot. "Okay," he said at last. "I'm going to trust you."

Zak grinned at him. "Thanks."

"And you don't want Control or anyone else to know what you're up to?" Bug added.

"That's the plan," said Zak.

Bug let out a long, deep sigh. "So, what happens now?"

"I'm going to pack a few things," said Zak. "Then I'm out of here."

Bug looked anxious. "You'll be careful, won't you?" he said.

"You know me," said Zak.

Bug nodded. "Yes," he said. "That's the problem."

Zak shoved a few things into his backpack. Before his Project 17 training, he would never have thought about carrying spare clothes, and he wasn't really expecting to need them now, but it was so ingrained in him now to be ready for any emergency that he did it almost without thinking.

He had pushed his Mob under his pillow, out of sight. He rummaged in a drawer and pulled out a watch. Without the Mob he'd need some way of telling the time.

He sat on the edge of his bed and tied his trainers. He had the burner phone in his pocket. He was almost ready to go.

The door to Zak's room opened suddenly. He almost hit the ceiling – but it was only Bug.

"I've been thinking," Bug said uneasily. "What if you don't come straight back? What do I do when people notice you're missing?"

"Cover for me?" Zak suggested, only half-serious.

Bug looked stricken. "I can't tell lies."

"No, of course not," said Zak. "If you're asked, tell them exactly what happened." He stood up, shrugging. "Chances are I'll be back before anyone even knows I've been out."

Bug held out his hand. "I thought this might come in useful," he said. "Just in case you get into trouble." It was a metal device, about the size of a small firework. Zak recognized it immediately. It was a handy little piece of Project 17 equipment called a Flash. Point it at an opponent, press the trigger and the Flash gives out a 10,000 watt burst of light – enough to temporarily blind anyone in the firing line.

Zak took it. "Thanks – good idea," he said. "I should go now."

Bug frowned. "Don't do anything stupid," he said, then he turned and left before Zak could reply.

Who – me?

Shouldering his backpack, Zak slipped out of his room and headed for one of the exit tunnels from the Fortress complex. A few minutes later, he was trotting along a dark, dank tunnel, lit dimly from above by early light filtering down through rusted iron gratings.

A metal ladder led him to an inspection hatch and the surface.

He glanced at his watch as he let the hatch clang shut. It was 05:12. He shivered in the cool early morning air and, with hunched shoulders, made his way into Vauxhall Bridge Road. It was only a ten-minute walk from here to Victoria station.

The concourse of Victoria train station was huge and brightly lit. Zak huddled on a cold metal bench, watching the commuters coming and going. When he'd arrived, most of the in-station shops had been closed. He'd sat quietly, watching the early morning activities of the station. A member of staff trundled by with a motorized floor cleaner. Shutters clanked as the shops were opened up. The smell of food filled the air. Trains came and went. Commuters swarmed as the morning rush hour began.

Zak looked at his watch. He'd already been here over an hour and still no phone call. It felt weird to be without his Mob. He hadn't realized how much he relied on it until it wasn't there. Somehow, leaving the Mob behind was the thing that made this whole business seem real.

Suddenly, the mobile phone rang. He pressed the green button and held it to his ear.

"Did you read your brother's file?" came Gabriel's voice.

"Yes."

"Are you ready to trust me now?"

Zak hesitated. He had one last question. "What's your codename?"

"I thought you'd have guessed," said Gabriel.

"Maybe I have," said Zak. "But I want you to tell me."

"Archangel." There was a pause. "It's time to make your mind up. Either you decide to trust me, or you don't."

"What do you want me to do?" asked Zak. "I'm not promising anything. I'm just *asking*, okay?"

"Go into the men's toilets," said Gabriel. "In the last cubicle on the left, you'll find a key taped to the back of the toilet-paper holder. The key is for a left-luggage locker. Open the locker and take out what you find. There will be instructions. If you decide to help me, you'll know what to do."

"When you call, it always shows 'number withheld'," said Zak. "Give me your number so I can call you back if I need to."

"I can't do that," said Gabriel. "If you get caught, I can't risk them tracing anything back to me."

Zak didn't like the sound of that at all. "If I get *caught*?" he asked. "What's that supposed to mean? Why would anyone catch me? Who even knows we're talking to each other?"

"No one," said Gabriel. "And I'm sure it's going to stay that way. But the mole has to be stopped, Zak. I'm sorry if this sounds selfish, but if something goes wrong and you're picked up, I need to know they can't use you to track me down."

"They?" asked Zak. "Who do you mean by '*they*'?"

"The mole reports to a man who works for a very big organization, Zak," said Gabriel. "Does the name World Serpent mean anything to you?"

"No. Should it?"

There was silence for a few moments. "Hunter is playing it close to his chest, I see," muttered Gabriel, in a voice so quiet that Zak barely heard him. "That's wise, I suppose. The fewer who know at the moment, the better."

"What are you talking about?" interrupted Zak.

"Switch the mobile off now, Zak," said Gabriel. "I'll call at midday. If you're on the train, we'll talk."

On the train? What train?

"Wait!" Zak half-yelled. "This is crazy! Why can't we just meet?"

"We will," said Gabriel. "But not yet. I'm not in the UK."

"So how have you set all this up?" asked Zak.

"Trusted friends," Gabriel replied. "People who have nothing to do with MI5 – people who could never be compromised by the mole. Turn the phone off, Zak." The line went dead.

Torn by doubt and confusion, Zak switched the phone off then got up and headed for the men's toilets.

Zak turned the key in the left-luggage locker and pulled the door open. There was a black holdall crammed inside. He yanked it out and closed the locker again.

He walked to a row of metal benches and sat down at one end, putting the holdall on his knees and undoing the zipper.

The bag wasn't heavy, and Zak got the impression

there wasn't much in it. He glanced around, checking that no one was watching him, then he opened it and stared inside. There were a bunch of papers at the bottom, tied with an elastic band.

He took the bundle out and pulled off the elastic band.

His eyes widened in surprise as he picked up a long slender piece of card.

It was a ticket for the Orient-Express, made out in the name of Zak Taylor. One way, London to Venice. Leaving from Victoria station at 09:00 that morning.

There was also a passport. He opened it and found he was staring at a picture of himself. Except that the name on the passport was Zak Taylor again.

There was a small folder with the circular logo of the Venice Simplon Orient-Express on the front. An Invitation to Board brochure. There was a folded map of Europe, showing the route the train would take across France, through the Swiss Alps, into Austria and then down to Venice, Italy. There were tourist brochures and cards explaining points of interest on the journey. There was an envelope with a number of banknotes inside.

Zak looked at the papers spread out on top of the holdall. He couldn't quite get his head around this.

Gabriel wanted him to take the Orient-Express to Venice? *One way?* A kind of subdued excitement began to fill him.

Venice. Wow!

No. This was crazy. No way was he going to get on that train.

But what if Gabriel was right? What if there really was a mole high up in British Intelligence? Not Colonel Hunter, Zak would never believe that. But someone the Colonel trusted? Someone *everyone* trusted. As Gabriel had said, if information was being given away by a traitor with access to the country's most closely guarded secrets, the results could be catastrophic.

Zak glanced at his watch.

It was 08:40.

He had exactly twenty minutes to make up his mind.

CHAPTER **FIVE**

FORTRESS.
09:12

Switchblade knocked on the door to Zak's room.

"You in there, Silver?" he called.

No answer.

He rapped his knuckles on the door again, more loudly this time. Quicksilver hadn't appeared in the canteen for breakfast. That wasn't so very unusual: people sometimes snacked in their rooms or slept in. Bug, for instance, never ate with the others. He always took his meals in his little frog-filled office.

But this was a school day and the first lesson was about to start. It was time for Silver to show himself.

"Hey, Silver, rise and shine!" Switchblade called, turning the handle and shoving the door open. "What's going on? Got lost under your duvet?"

Switch marched into the room. The bed was empty. The covers were rumpled, but not in the way he'd have expected if Silver had just jumped out in a wild panic at finding he was late.

He pushed open the door of the en-suite bathroom.

No one there. He entered and ran a finger around the inside of the basin. It was dry. Obviously it hadn't been used recently.

Switchblade walked out again, scanning the main room for some clue as to what was going on.

Something was definitely off.

He took out his Mob and speed dialled Quicksilver.

Silver's familiar, bass-heavy ringtone sounded from close by. Muffled by something. Switchblade strode to the bed and jerked the pillow aside. Zak's Mob lay there, lit up and ringing.

Okay.

This was getting seriously strange now.

*

Zak gazed out of the train window as the Kent countryside sped past, all trees and low rolling hills and green and brown fields, interrupted by the occasional small town.

He was in the plush dining car of the Orient-Express. He had a table all to himself and he was having a much-needed brunch. He had been so preoccupied with the weird events of the past few hours that he hadn't realized how hungry he was until the food had begun to arrive.

Around him, couples and families were busy eating, as smart waiters glided and hovered about, polite and attentive.

Zak had been shown to his seat by a steward in a blue jacket and a bowtie. The man had greeted him as he had climbed onto the train.

"Mr Taylor, welcome aboard. Your father left explicit instructions that you are to be looked after with special care. Please, let me take your luggage. I'll drop it in your cabin then show you to your table."

Bemused, Zak had handed over the holdall and his backpack.

For 'father' read 'Gabriel', he assumed.

The train had departed on the dot of nine o'clock. It had taken a while to be rid of the dull grey London scenery, but by the time Zak was tucking into his food, they were whizzing towards the Kent coast at over 130 kilometres an hour.

As he sipped orange juice through a straw and spread strawberry jam on yet another warm roll, he was still trying to come to terms with the decision he had made in getting on this train in the first place.

His brain had told him not to do it – his *brain* told him to go straight to Colonel Hunter and spill everything. But some powerful and determined instinct was urging him to trust Gabriel – or Archangel, or whatever he was called – to trust him and to help him root out the mole who was handing over vital secrets to terrorists. If doing that jeopardized his relationship with Colonel Hunter and Project 17, then he'd have to deal with that when he got back. But, right now, he knew he needed to see this through to the end.

I really hope I made the right choice, he thought to himself as he watched cows glide past in a sunny meadow. *If I've messed up, I can kiss goodbye to my Project 17 career for sure.* He looked at his watch. *They'll have noticed I'm missing by now. Poor Bug. I wish he hadn't got caught up in this. I hope he doesn't get into trouble.*

He picked up the Invitation to Board brochure and had another look at the proposed itinerary.

The train would take its passengers to Folkestone, where they would transfer to a special coach that would carry them through the Channel Tunnel to Calais. Once in France, they would board the European Orient-Express, which was apparently made up of luxurious continental wagon-lits.

Zak had had to ask what a wagon-lit was.

A sleeping car, it turned out. He had a double one all to himself. Gabriel must have been pretty sure Zak would go for this, considering how much money he had spent on the trip – not to mention the cost of that fake passport.

Gabriel's voice was running on a loop in his head. *The mole has to be stopped, Zak. I'm sorry if this sounds selfish, but if something goes wrong and you're picked up, I need to know they can't use you to track me down.* By 'they', Zak assumed he meant the terrorists.

A cold thrill of fear ran down Zak's spine as the full impact of what he was doing hit him. The mole they were hunting down reported to an international terrorist organization. Terrorists kill people. That's what they do. What exactly had he let himself in for? He was here without Colonel Hunter's permission. He had no back-up. He was alone on a train, in a foreign country, teamed with someone who so far was only a voice on the end of a phone.

Dangerous.

Crazy dangerous.

He needed to think about something else before he got totally freaked out. He opened the Invitation to Board brochure again and carried on reading.

The train would whisk them to Paris by seven o'clock in the evening local time. There would be a three-hour stopover before the train carried on through the night into the Swiss Alps and on to the Austrian city of Innsbruck for breakfast. After a short break, the train would then head south-east into Italy and make its way to the final destination of Venice by late afternoon.

I must be totally mental to be doing this, Zak thought, imagining Colonel Hunter's angry face and what he might say: "You left Fortress without my permission in order to do *what*?"

Control is going to kill me for sure if it turns out there's no mole. He'll kill me, and then throw me out of Project 17, and then kill me some more.

Unless, of course, Colonel Hunter *was* the mole?

No! Whatever kind of craziness he was heading into, Zak would not believe that. Never. And if Gabriel tried to convince him otherwise, Zak would be gone. No more hints and clues and mysterious phone calls. It would be over.

✳

FORTRESS.

Zak's unauthorized absence had been noticed. Big time.

The day's normal activities had been suspended: lessons cancelled, training sessions brought to an abrupt halt. All agents not in the field had been gathered in the main briefing room. There was a subdued buzz of inquisitive voices while they waited for Colonel Hunter to arrive.

Silver's done a runner.

No, he's been abducted.

No, he had an argument with Control and stormed out.

Everyone knew Quicksilver was missing – but no one knew a thing about what had happened; except for one of them, and he wasn't saying anything.

Bug sat a little apart from the others, his head down as he worked some mind-shredding maths game on his tablet computer. Switchblade and Wildcat were huddled together, talking under their breath, trying to make sense of Zak's disappearance.

Colonel Hunter strode in and the room went silent.

"As you all know, Agent Quicksilver has been reported missing," said the Colonel without preamble. "I've had time to go over last night's CCTV footage. There was a glitch in the system for a few minutes, when some of the cameras developed a fault and no images were recorded. Bug has looked into this and he's sure this was a simple electronic problem that quickly repaired itself."

Switchblade looked over at Bug. That kid was never good with large numbers of people, but Switch got the feeling Bug was even more nervous than usual. He didn't even look up when his name was mentioned.

"Footage from zero-four-forty-five shows Quicksilver leaving his room with a backpack and making his way to P17 exit Delta 5," the Colonel continued.

Switch ticked off the exits in his mind. Delta 5 led to Aylesford Street – near Vauxhall Bridge. Why would Silver go there?

"Perhaps the most significant element of this is the fact that Quicksilver did not take his Mob," said the Colonel.

"Could he have forgotten it?" someone asked.

"That's a possibility," Colonel Hunter replied. "But my feeling is that he left it behind deliberately so he could not be tracked."

Every Mob had a built-in GPS tracker app that could not be turned off. If they had their Mob on them, agents could be followed in real time whether they were walking down Oxford Street in the middle of London or trekking across the Sahara desert. No Project 17 agent would ever be out of contact so long as he carried his Mob.

"At the moment I'm classing this as a Code Orange," said Hunter. Orange was the second-highest level of alert. "If nothing is heard from Quicksilver within a few hours, that will change to Code Red, and at some point I'll have to issue a Codeword Rogue."

Switchblade knew very well what Codeword Rogue meant. It was the same level of alarm that Control had initiated when the Project 17 agent called Ballerina had turned traitor. A chill ran through Switchblade's body. Did the Colonel think Silver had betrayed them?

"Dismissed," the Colonel said sharply. "You can go back to your normal duties, unless you hear otherwise from me."

The agents got up and filed out of the room.

"Bug?" Colonel Hunter called. The boy stopped in the doorway. Switch was close behind him with Wildcat.

"Yes, Control?"

"I'd like you to double-check that system fault," the Colonel said. "Make sure it's nothing we need to worry about."

Bug nodded and shuffled off.

Switchblade hesitated in the doorway, looking at the

Colonel. "I'd trust Quicksilver with my life, Control," he said. "If he's gone rogue, I'd bet there's a good reason for it."

Colonel Hunter looked closely at him but, as ever, it was impossible to tell what he was thinking behind the steely grey eyes. "I'll take that into consideration, Switchblade," he said.

"Is there anything in his room?" asked Wildcat. "Any clue as to what might have set him off?"

The Colonel shook his head. "There was a phone call yesterday," he said. "A package had arrived for him at the children's home where he used to live. I gave him leave to go and collect it. I called the home this morning and I was told he picked the package up mid-afternoon. It was apparently a padded envelope postmarked France."

"Then there must have been something in the package that he needed to deal with," said Switch. "Something personal."

"I'm allowing for that possibility," said the Colonel. "But no matter what it was, he knows better than to absent himself without leave or explanation." He took his Mob from his pocket and checked the time. "If Quicksilver hasn't made contact soon, I'll have to call the Codeword Rogue. The Director General of MI5 and the Home Secretary will be informed, and from then on Quicksilver's fate will be out of my hands."

"He'll be thrown out of Project 17?" asked Wildcat.

"That's quite certain," said Colonel Hunter. "But unless he has a very convincing reason for his absence, being discontinued as a Project 17 agent will be the least of his worries."

He stalked away, leaving Switchblade and Wildcat staring uneasily at one another.

If he didn't get in touch within the next few hours, Silver was for the chop.

FORTRESS.
11.20
AN OFFICE FULL OF FROGS.

Bug sat in his chair, chewing his lip and staring blankly ahead. He watched the digital time display slowly changing. At what point would he have to go to Control and tell him the whole story?

Soon, for sure. He didn't want a Codeword Rogue being called on Quicksilver. That would be a total disaster.

He wished Quicksilver would get in touch and bring this craziness to an end. He really liked Silver and he trusted him – but there was a limit to what he could do for him. Bug was afraid that he had already overstepped the mark by faking that glitch in the system to wipe the CCTV footage of Silver in his office.

The click of the door being opened was as loud as a gunshot in his head.

He twisted his head, expecting to see Control.

Why did you fake the CCTV glitch, Bug? Are you and Quicksilver working against me?

No! It's nothing like that.

Bug's breath came out in a relieved gasp. It was Switchblade.

"Have you heard anything?" Switch asked, coming into the office.

"No, nothing," mumbled Bug, looking up at him.

Switch walked over to the work station and leaned against the edge, arms folded, his blue eyes boring into Bug's face.

"Do you know anything about Silver's little walkabout?" Switch asked.

"Nothing," Bug repeated, blinking rapidly.

Switch's eyes narrowed. "Why are you lying to me?"

"I'm not!"

Switch shook his head. "You're the world's worst liar, Bug," he said. "You have a really obvious *tell*."

Bug stared at him. "A what?"

"A *tell*," said Switch. "It's something you do when you're not telling the truth. Your blink rate skyrockets."

Bug tried to force his eyes to stay open. "You're making that up!"

Switch shook his head. "Why are you covering for Silver?" he asked. "What's he doing?"

"I don't know anything!" *Blink. Blink. Blink.*

"Do you know what will happen when Control calls the Codeword Rogue protocol?" asked Switch. "Do you know what kind of trouble Silver will be in?" Switch took a deep breath. "Listen, Bug, I won't run to Control with this, but you have to tell me what you know."

That was it for Bug. He couldn't keep it up any longer. "I don't know what's going on," he blurted, feeling relieved that he had someone to talk to at last. "I found him in here late last night, after everyone else was in bed." And so Bug told Switchblade everything that had happened.

"You let him walk out – just like that?" gasped Switchblade. "Bug! That's crazy. It could all be lies. Silver could be in real danger. For all you know, he could be on a plane over the Atlantic right now, bound and gagged and heading for some terrorist hideout in South America."

"No," said Bug, sitting up and typing on his keyboard. "He isn't. I know that for sure."

"How?" snapped Switch.

"Because I slipped a tracker onto him without him noticing," said Bug. "Look!" He tapped a final key and one of the plasma screens burst into life.

It was a satellite image of a big chunk of countryside. There were woods and fields through which roads and railways lines snaked.

A small red light pulsed in the middle of the image. Bug pressed some more keys and the image zoomed in.

"He's there," said Bug, pointing to the screen. "Silver is right there!"

CHAPTER **SIX**

FRANCE.
THE ORIENT-EXPRESS, SOMEWHERE
BETWEEN CALAIS AND ABBEVILLE.

Zak's private cabin was on the small side, but it felt as luxurious as a five-star hotel room. He was leaning back into a large sofa, his feet resting on a padded stool, drinking cola with ice and watching the French countryside slide past under a clear blue sky. There was a door to one side that opened onto a neat little cabinet with a washbasin and hot and cold running water. There was also a bell he could ring for twenty-four-hour steward service.

Anyone watching Zak might have thought he was having the time of his life. But there was a deep frown on his face, and he was hardly aware of the scenery as the train thundered south towards Paris.

The further he got from Fortress, the more uneasy he was becoming. He was Project 17's newest recruit. Sure, he'd been on a couple of missions, but never on his own, never without an older and more experienced agent to watch his back.

He no longer had any doubts about Gabriel, but he was beginning to wonder whether he was up to this mission. What if he messed up? What if he made some stupid newbie error and the mole found out he was being targeted? The mole could cover his tracks. He might never be found. He could carry on betraying his country. And all because of some dumb mistake by idiot Agent Quicksilver.

He took the phone out of his pocket, his fingers hesitating over the pad.

Call Colonel Hunter. Tell him everything – he'll know what to do. He'll send help. Get yourself out of this mess while you still can.

What were you thinking, going off on your own

like this?

Are you crazy?

The phone rang.

It was exactly noon.

Zak hesitated. It was now or never. Follow the mission, or back out while he still could?

He picked up. "Are you still with me, Zak?" asked Gabriel's voice.

"Yes. I'm on the train," Zak replied.

"Trust me, I know how hard this must be for you," said Gabriel. "You're thinking you've made a big mistake, aren't you? You're thinking you just want to go back to Fortress."

"Something like that," Zak responded guardedly.

"You've come this far, Zak," said Gabriel. "Do you really want to quit?"

"I'm not going to quit," Zak said firmly. "So, what happens next?"

"We'll meet at the Gare de l'Est railway station in Paris," said Gabriel. "I'll be there when the train pulls in. We'll get together and I'll explain everything to you then."

"Explain some of it now," said Zak. "You said you needed me because I was quick and I was good at free running. How about a few more details? How are speed and free running going to help find the mole?"

"The only way to flush out the mole is via his European contact," Gabriel said slowly. "His contact is an official in a large international merchant bank in Venice. I need someone who can get in and out of the building where he works very quickly." His voice took on a hard edge. "Listen, Zak, I'm telling you stuff that could lead directly to me if you blab. Stuff that could get me killed, do you understand?"

"Yes, I understand," said Zak.

"The mole's codename is Talpa," said Gabriel. "It's a kind of joke, you see?"

"It is?"

"Talpa is Italian for *mole*."

"Oh, okay. Yes, that's hilarious," Zak said dryly.

"The mole's controller is known as Padrone," Gabriel continued. "That means *master* in Italian."

"And how does me being good at free running fit into this?" Zak asked.

"I'm not giving you the details of that now," said Gabriel. "I'll meet you in Paris and we can discuss the exact procedures of the operation while we travel."

Zak said nothing.

"Chill out, Zak," came the voice. "Remember, I've read your file. This whole thing should be totally in your comfort zone. I'll see you soon. Leave the phone on this time, just in case I need to call again."

Gabriel hung up.

Zak stared at the phone for a long time. He was committed now. He'd see it through to the end. He just hoped that Gabriel hadn't made a huge mistake in choosing him.

A knock sounded on his cabin door.

"Mr Taylor?" came the steward's voice. "Lunch is being served in the restaurant car whenever you're ready."

"Thanks," Zak called. "I'm coming."

He heaved himself up off the sofa. He should eat. It might even help take his mind off his self-doubt.

FORTRESS.
CONTROL'S OFFICE.

Colonel Hunter put down the phone. He was frowning and his face wore an expression of mingled anger and concern. He didn't like having to field phone calls from William Kent in the office of the Director General of MI5. Especially not calls enquiring whether a missing agent of Project 17 had been located yet.

Protocol demanded that he advise the Home

Secretary and the MI5 chief about the problem in his department, but they were waiting for his final word before setting the Rogue protocols in motion. The high-security procedures would involve the issue of an All Points Warning that would mean a crackdown at all airports, seaports and international railway stations. And if that didn't flush him out, the net would be widened to include Europe and the Americas. One way or another, Quicksilver would be hunted down and dragged back to Fortress in handcuffs. His career would be over. His life would be changed forever.

A ping rang out on Colonel Hunter's computer and the screen lit up to show Colonel Pearce's face.

"Has the boy been found, Colonel?" she asked crisply.

"No," Colonel Hunter replied, slightly irritated by the call and in no mood to chat with his counterpart in Citadel.

"I'm ready to give you whatever assistance you may require," said Colonel Pearce. "You only have to ask, Peter."

"Thank you, Margaret, but I have things under control for the time being." Colonel Hunter forced a smile as he broke the vid-link. The moment Colonel Pearce's face vanished, Colonel Hunter brought both fists crashing down on his desk in frustration.

Where was Quicksilver? What was he doing?

He had the definite feeling that Bug knew something, but he didn't want to have to call Bug in here and force him to talk – not until the last possible second. If Bug volunteered information about Quicksilver, Colonel Hunter could be lenient with him. If the information had to be dragged out of him . . . well, the Colonel had no wish to lose two agents over this incident, not if he could help it.

His intercom beeped.

"You have a call from Rampart and another from the Home Office," came his secretary's voice.

"Hold both calls for the moment," said the Colonel.

He tapped his keyboard and a CCTV link appeared, showing Bug in his small circular office. Working normally, as far as Colonel Hunter could tell.

He pursed his lips, his finger hovering over the key that would open a com-link to Bug.

A ping announced the arrival of another vid-link. This time it was from Lieutenant Colonel McDermott of Bastion. McDermott had never approved of Project 17 – he often referred to it as *playschool* or the *crèche*. His bulldog face glowered at Colonel Hunter.

"I would have expected you to call the Codeword Rogue by now, Colonel," he said.

"I'm actively considering all my options, thank you," said Colonel Hunter. "You'll be told of my decision in due course."

Lieutenant Colonel McDermott snorted. "You know my opinion," he said. "I've said from the start that your little band of adolescents would let you down sooner or later. If the Home Secretary had taken my advice, Project 17 would have been closed down a long time ago – or handed over to someone with a firmer hand. You're too lax with them, Hunter. Project 17 should be run by someone with a firmer grasp of discipline."

"Thank you for your input, Lieutenant Colonel," said Colonel Hunter, with icy politeness. "Your comments will be taken under advisement."

He broke the link, his face thunderous.

Where was Quicksilver?

Madeleine Farris winced as she heard another thump from Colonel Hunter's office. She had the uneasy feeling he'd just snatched something from his desk and thrown it across the room. She hoped it wasn't anything breakable. She'd been his secretary for three years and she'd never seen him so angry.

Strange that, of all his agents, Quicksilver could get

under his skin like this. When Control had learned of Ballerina's treachery, his anger had been intense but perfectly calm. This was different. She glanced at the intercom. Two lights blinked red. One from John Mallin, the Home Secretary's PPS, the other from Rampart.

Both would normally be put through immediately. Both were on hold.

Her door opened a fraction and Bug peered in at her.

She shook her head at him, but he came in anyway.

"Is Control free?" he asked hesitantly, his big eyes anxious under his fringe.

"You don't want to go in there right now, Bug," she warned. "This isn't a good time."

Bug gnawed his lip, staring at the Colonel's door.

"Try later," Madeleine Farris recommended, lowering her voice. "Unless you want your head bitten off."

Bug looked at the door for a few more seconds then turned and walked out of the room.

The Orient-Express had pulled in under the great arched glass and steel roof of the Gare de l'Est in Paris. Announcements rang through the carriages in French and English.

"The Orient-Express will remain at the station for

three hours, ladies and gentlemen. Please feel free to leave the train and see some of the wonderful sights of the City of Light. While you enjoy yourselves, your stewards will convert your cabins for the night. Please return to the train in plenty of time for our departure at ten o'clock."

Zak opened the window of his cabin and leaned out, watching the people milling about on the platform. He wondered which of them was Gabriel. Would he recognize him – one agent to another?

The train emptied, and gradually the activity on the platform dwindled to a few people standing about chatting and some walking towards the exit.

Zak frowned. Was Gabriel waiting for the crowds to disappear before coming aboard? That made sense. He sat on the sofa, looking at his watch.

The train had been standing here for over ten minutes.

Where was Gabriel?

He took the phone out of his pocket. It was switched off. He must have done it automatically when that last call with Gabriel ended. He quickly activated the phone. It rang immediately.

"I told you to keep it on!" Gabriel sounded annoyed.

"Sorry," said Zak. "I forgot. Where are you?"

"Have you blabbed?" snapped Gabriel.

"What are you talking about?" Zak was shocked by the violent tone in Gabriel's voice.

"Have you told anyone about this mission?" said Gabriel. "Have you been in contact with Fortress? Hunter? Anyone at all?"

"Of course not," said Zak, becoming alarmed. "What's happened?"

"I was in the station," said Gabriel in a hushed, rapid voice. "But I saw some people I thought I recognized. People who mustn't know I'm here."

"What people?" asked Zak, standing and peering up and down the platform.

"Some of Padrone's gang," said Gabriel. "I think they must have tracked me here somehow. It's not safe for us to meet on the train any more."

"So what do I do?" asked Zak. His worst fears were coming true. The terrorists were moving in on them already.

"Get off the train and go to the Eiffel Tower," said Gabriel. "I'll meet you outside the Jules Verne restaurant on the second level. Leave your phone on this time, in case I need to call you again."

The line went dead.

Zak sat down heavily, shocked by the call and uncertain what to make of the fact that Gabriel was being tailed. Did this mean *he* was in danger too? Did Padrone's people know about him – what he looked like, why he was here?

His training kicked in quickly. He stood up again and snatched his holdall and backpack from the luggage rack. He stuffed the backpack into the holdall, and glanced around quickly to check he hadn't left anything behind.

No. Everything he'd brought with him was in the holdall now.

He opened the cabin door and moved out into the corridor. A tall man in a bright blue uniform barred his way.

"Hello, young man. Off to see the sights?" said the man.

"Yes," Zak said, his senses tingling, his eyes searching the man for any sign of a weapon. If Gabriel had been compromised, Padrone's men might also know about their planned meeting aboard the train.

"Enjoy yourself," said the man, stepping aside and allowing Zak to pass. "Remember to be back by ten o'clock."

"Thanks, I will," said Zak. He moved towards the open door and jumped down onto the platform. He walked rapidly to the exit.

What was going to happen now? If Gabriel had been seen at the station, would they have to find some other way of getting to Venice together? Maybe the fact that Padrone's men had followed Gabriel here meant that the whole operation would have to be terminated. The mole would be free to carry on spilling Britain's most important secrets to the terrorists. Thousands of lives would be in danger.

No. Giving up now wasn't an option. Doubts and fears needed to be put aside. This mission had to succeed. There was no other option.

CHAPTER **SEVEN**

"Trocadero," called the driver as the bus slowed to a halt.

The doors hissed open and Zak grabbed his holdall.

"*Merci beaucoup*," he called as he jumped off. School French. Who knew it could come in handy?

Ahead of him, towering up beyond the Trocadero Gardens and the River Seine, he saw the tall spire of the Eiffel Tower, straddling its concrete plinth on heavy iron legs.

A helpful English-speaking woman at the information desk of the railway station had told him how to get here.

"It is very easy; take the number thirty-two bus in the direction of Porte d'Auteuil. It will take no more than thirty minutes. You will know when you get there. The tower is not easy to miss."

She hadn't been kidding, thought Zak as he made his way alongside the long sloping lawns of the gardens. The huge iron landmark absolutely dominated the city, stabbing up into the sky like some kind of weird steampunk skyrocket. It was way more impressive in real life than in any of the pictures he'd seen.

He walked through the crowds, hearing people speaking French, understanding virtually none of it. So much for school French, after all. To his right, an oblong lake of blue water sent fountains spurting into the sky. The lake was lined with bronze and stone statues, the lawns dotted with strolling people.

But he was too preoccupied with his upcoming meeting with Gabriel to enjoy sightseeing. He just wanted to finally come face-to-face with the man behind the voice. The man he'd risked everything to help. And once they were together, he wanted to get on with the mission and make sure that the treacherous mole got everything he deserved.

Zak joined the crowds crossing the busy main road and walked with them onto the bridge that spanned the River Seine. Pleasure boats cruised on the greeny-brown water, leaving white wakes.

There was a festive atmosphere around the tower. People lined up for fast food and gifts at the shops at its four feet. Others sat on benches or in the grass on the far side, picnicking or strolling arm in arm. He joined the queue at the ticket booth. The great metal structure loomed over him, a vast lacework of iron girders that cast cool dark shadows.

What had Gabriel said? Meet outside the Jules Verne restaurant on the second level. Zak rummaged in his holdall, remembering the envelope he had seen among the various documents; the envelope with Euros in it.

He bought a ticket for the lift to the second level then joined another queue at one of the huge concrete bases and waited patiently as the tourists and visitors shuffled noisily and excitedly into the yellow double-decker lift.

Zak pushed aboard, not liking the crowds that surrounded him, wary of the doors closing on them, hemming him in. If one of Padrone's men was in here with him, he had nowhere to run, no way of escaping.

The lift began to rise up the girdered leg of the tower. Through the large window he could see a stairway zigzagging alongside the lift. Maybe he should

have taken the stairs? At least that would have given him options.

The lift stopped at the first level. Some people got off and others climbed in. Zak glanced from face to face, wondering if one of the anonymous young men might be Gabriel, worrying that one of them might be there for more sinister reasons.

Don't start getting paranoid, he told himself. Good advice, but it didn't stop his heart pattering in his chest and it didn't lessen that horrible feeling of being watched. The lift glided in a long smooth curve up to the second level. The doors opened and Zak got out, surrounded by animated tourists, chattering loudly, pushing this way and that.

He walked over to the rail and joined the row of people gazing out over the panorama of Paris. It was worth a look! Blocks of grey buildings stretched away into the hazy distance, threaded with trees and gardens and wide, traffic-filled boulevards. The sun was low in the sky behind him, throwing deep shadows over the symmetrical lawns and pathways of the long expanse of the Champ de Mars. He leaned further over the edge, staring at the ground, so far below that the people moving about down there looked too small to be real.

He was on high alert as he made his way to the Jules Verne restaurant. There was a queue of people waiting to get in. He gazed through the tinted windows. It looked very exclusive.

He turned, his back to the windows, his eyes scanning the crowds, watching for anything out of the ordinary. Project 17 training had taught him how to 'scope' a crowd, how to look for the little 'tells'. Shifty eyes that look away fast when you notice them. Buttoned-up coats that could hide a concealed weapon. People hanging around nearby for just that little bit too long. Men on their own who ignore the magnificent views. People who arrive together then split up. There were plenty of tells – but so far Zak hadn't seen any of them.

He assumed that Gabriel knew what he looked like; that Gabriel would approach him. He looked at his watch.

It was a few minutes past eight o'clock.

Where was Gabriel?

20:54
THE EIFFEL TOWER, PARIS.

Zak grew more irritated and frustrated as the minutes ticked slowly by. No Gabriel. No phone call. Nothing.

The sun had almost gone now and it seemed as though a million lights were glimmering in the gathering darkness of the city below, the busy roads picked out in a soft amber glow, and major buildings shining brightly.

But the lights of Paris did nothing to alter Zak's mood. He was stranded here in a foreign city with only a handful of Euros to his name and a one-way ticket to Venice in his bag. What if Gabriel had been taken? What if Padrone's men had got to him? Did that mean they would be coming for Zak too?

I'll give him till nine o'clock. Six more minutes.

But then what?

Lights had come on up on the second level of the tower, throwing a confusion of shadows over the shifting crowds. Gradually Zak began to get the feeling that a couple of men were watching him. Two ordinary men in casual clothes, hanging around, taking photos, apparently doing nothing more sinister than enjoying the view. Yeah, right! They blended in perfectly with the other tourists and sightseers, but there was something about them, something that made his Project 17 antennae twitchy.

It was as if they were deliberately *not* looking in his direction. As if they were avoiding any chance of eye contact with him – although he was certain they had spotted him the moment they had appeared up here.

In training, this was called 'Locate and Wait'. Find your target, keep close, but don't draw attention to yourself. Not until it's time to strike.

Zak shoved his hand into the holdall and rummaged around until he closed his fingers around the cool metal tube of the Flash. He drew it out and slipped it into his pocket. Best to be ready – just in case. *Or am I going crazy?* Maybe they were just two ordinary guys minding their own business.

After all, how could anyone make the link between him and Gabriel? He was just a fourteen-year-old boy. Out on the town. Seeing the sights of Paris. An innocent kid.

All the same . . .

His mobile rang.

"Where are you?" spat Zak, not giving Gabriel time to speak. "I've been . . . "

Gabriel's voice was an urgent bark. "I've been made. Get out of there. Get back to the train. Use Foxhunt Rules. I'll try to meet you on board. If not, I'll get to Venice some other way and find you there."

Panic seared through Zak's body. "Wait . . . !" he gasped, but he was silenced by a sharp command.

"*Go!*"

The line went dead.

Foxhunt Rules. Zak knew exactly what that meant. Foxhunt Rules were the tactics used by agents when they were deep in enemy territory – when their lives were at risk.

He glanced towards the two men. One of them was watching him now over the other's shoulder. His eyes were cold and hard. His lips moved but he was too far away for Zak to hear what he had said. The other man turned around. His face was impassive, emotionless. But the look in his eyes was deadly.

Zak edged away from them, pressing his way through the crowds, slipping around the corner. The tourists were in no hurry, but Zak was. He zigzagged in among them, trying to put distance between himself and the men.

A group of school kids was gathered around the top of the stairs. A teacher was yelling to make herself heard over their excited racket. Zak would have to go right through them.

He heard the sound of the lift doors opening close by. He turned, pushing into the jostling mass of people boarding the lift.

He felt something hard jab him in the back. A hand came down on his shoulder. A voice hissed close to his ear: "*Non dicono nulla. Venga con me.*" He had no idea what it meant, but the hard object was pressed more firmly into his back now and the hand on his shoulder was pulling him away from the lift entrance.

He had a bad feeling that the thing in his back was a gun.

The man led him to where the second man was standing, in a corner of the wide walkway where girders obstructed the view of the city and there were fewer people.

The second man smiled, but his eyes were blank. "*Dove si trova?*" he asked in a quiet, almost friendly voice. Zak stared at him, guessing he was speaking Italian, his mind busy with escape options.

The man's eyes narrowed. "*Où est-il?*"

Zak knew enough French to understand that question. *Where is he?* The men wanted to know where Gabriel was.

"I'm sorry," Zak said, gazing at the man with wide, innocent eyes. "But I don't understand what you're saying."

"*Cosa sta dicendo?*" hissed the man at his back.

"*Inglese,*" muttered the other man. He frowned at Zak. "You are English?" he said in a thick Italian accent.

"I am," Zak said cheerfully. Act dumb until you come

up with a plan. "I'm here on a school trip. Can you ask your friend to stop poking me in the back – it's really uncomfortable."

The man glanced around, as though checking that no one was paying attention to them. "Where is he?" he asked softly.

"I really don't know what you mean," said Zak. He had no room for doubt now – somehow these two men knew he was there to meet Gabriel. He'd worry about *how* they knew some other time. He had more urgent things to deal with.

The man leaned forwards, his eyes black under heavy brows. "You *do* know what I mean," he whispered. "You tell us or we take you to a quiet place where you will talk. *Capito?* You understand me? You will be made to tell us what we want to know."

Zak looked into the man's eyes, pushing down his fear, refusing to be strong-armed by these men, no matter how dangerous they were. Every sinew and muscle in his body was tensed. When he acted, it needed to be sudden and startling. And he had to make sure that no one nearby got hurt.

"Okay," he said, making his voice sound defeated. "I know what you want. I can bring him here." He gestured towards his pocket. "I've got a phone – I can call him."

"Do it," said the man.

Zak pushed his hand into his pocket. His stomach was knotted, his throat so tight he could hardly breathe. He closed his fingers around the Flash.

He pulled out the Flash and twisted on his heels, aiming it in the gunman's face and pressing the trigger. At the exact moment that 10,000 watts of raw white light exploded out of the device, he lifted his leg and brought the edge of his shoe raking down the other man's shin and then stamped with all his weight on his foot.

The gunman tottered backwards with a shriek, the gun falling from his fingers as he brought his hands up to his face. The other man let out a bellow of pain and dropped to his knees.

Catching the gun one-handed as it spun through the air, Zak darted away from them and dodged into the crowd. Other people were screaming and shouting – a few tourists behind the gunman had also got the full force of the Flash in their faces, and others were pushing forwards to see what had happened.

Zak nipped between them, shoving the gun into his holdall. Someone jogged up against him and the Flash was jolted from his hand. He saw it go skittering across the floor. He lunged for it, but a foot caught it and kicked it further away.

Forget it. You don't have time!

He headed for the stairs. The gang of school kids was gone. A few people were climbing and descending, but there was clear space between them. Zak hesitated for a fraction of a second at the top of the stairs, then he just went for it.

He leaped down the first ten steps, landing on both feet, springing onwards and downwards, angling himself sideways to avoid a startled-looking elderly couple who clung to one another as he barrelled past them.

"*Excusez-moi!*" he yelled, hitting the foot of the stairs at speed as people scattered out of his way with angry shouts. His momentum sent him hurtling towards the brown metal cage that enclosed the stairs. He twisted in the air, bending his knees and lifting his legs so that his feet struck against the steel mesh. Kicking out, he changed direction and headed for the next plunging staircase.

More people! He had to be careful not to hurt anyone. "*Excusez-moi! Merci!*" he yelled. Not terribly helpful, but at least it warned them he was coming.

He jumped onto the thin metal handrail, standing sideways with his feet together. Spreading his arms for balance, he slid down the rail, picking up even more speed as he went. People stared and shouted. He landed on his toes and fingertips, then turned, his eyes instinctively scoping out the obstacles and possibilities as he flung himself down the next stairway.

He was in the zone now, his brain totally focused on the way ahead, his body moving smoothly and quickly, jumping to the left and the right to avoid crashing into anyone, his brain already working on problems several metres ahead.

Parents with two small children were just ahead of him. He leaped, tucking his legs under, soaring right over them, throwing one foot out to catch the handrail so that he was spun sideways to avoid hitting more people. *Bang!* Down to the next level. Grab the rail to swing himself around, and down another flight.

He came sprinting out at ground level, threading through the evening crowds, not even panting.

In the zone.

He ran without thinking, not caring where he was headed, just trying to put as much space as possible between himself and those two men.

He darted across the main road and ran along a tree-lined walkway above the river. Below he could see car parks and jetties where pleasure boats were moored. The raised walkway followed the long curve of the river. Zak glanced over his shoulder. The Eiffel Tower was lit up now from top to bottom, shining brightly against the dark sky as though it were made of solid gold.

Wow!

Never mind, wow. What are you doing? What's the plan?

Gabriel said to get back aboard the Orient Express.

Are you sure you want to do that?

Yes. Yes, I am.

But how to get to the station in time? He only had about forty minutes until the Orient-Express was due to leave. Would the same bus get him there quickly enough? He wasn't sure. Then, as though in answer to an unspoken prayer, Zak saw a red and yellow Métro sign up ahead. The Paris equivalent of the London Underground train system. *Spectacular!*

A couple of minutes later, he was in the Champ de Mars Tour Eiffel station, scanning a map of the Métro. He saw that he needed to take the RER C line train to St-Michel, then pick up Métro Line 4 to Gare de l'Est.

He went onto the platform, still watchful, still on alert.

Foxhunt Rules.

His train pulled in. He stood back as people got on and off. There was no sign of the two men from the Tower, but he had no idea of how many people Padrone might have sent in pursuit of Gabriel. Just those two? Four? A dozen? And he couldn't figure out how they'd linked him to Gabriel. Had they monitored the calls on the burner phone? And even if they had, how had that told them what he looked like?

The doors of the train began to close. At the last possible moment, Zak leaped aboard, the doors closing right behind him. As the train began to move, he stared through the window, looking for anything suspicious.

Nothing. All good. So far.

At the first stop, he got off the train. Again, just as the doors were closing, he sprang back aboard. Anyone following him would need to be quick on their feet.

He looked at the time. It was almost half past nine. He had only thirty minutes to get back to the Orient-Express. It was going to be tight.

He hit the Gare de l'Est with two minutes to spare. Ignoring the surprised looks of other people on the concourse, he sprinted at top speed for the platform.

He heard a whistle blowing. A man in uniform stepped in front of him, one hand raised.

"Arrêt! Arrêt!" the man shouted.

Stop! Stop!

No way.

Zak jinked past him, easily avoiding the man's grabbing arms. The barrier was down, but he vaulted over it without breaking pace.

The train was just pulling out of the station. Zak raced along the platform, chasing after the elegant blue-liveried last carriage.

It was picking up speed, drawing away from him.

He clicked into the zone again, his feet skimming the concrete, his arms pumping. Finally he drew up alongside the train. He flung out a hand and caught hold of the chrome rail alongside the door of the last carriage.

One last push and his feet were on the metal runner. He scrambled up, shouldered in through the elegant wooden door and found himself facing his steward in the corridor of the train.

"Welcome aboard, Mr Taylor," the man said with a smile, looking as though nothing out of the ordinary had just happened. "That was a close thing. Maybe you left it a *little* on the late side?"

Zak nodded. "I think you're right," he said. "I lost track of the time."

"It's easily done," said the steward, standing aside. "Your cabin has been made ready for the night. I hope you sleep well."

"Thanks," said Zak, edging past him. "I think I probably will."

He made his way along the train to his cabin. The sofa had been converted into two bunk beds against the wall. A soft light came from the lamp on the side table.

Zak closed the door behind him. Kicking off his shoes, he threw himself onto the bottom bunk and listened to the rhythmic rumble and clunk of the train as it gathered speed.

He closed his eyes, his brain still spinning.

A close thing.

It certainly had been. In more ways than that guy could ever have imagined!

CHAPTER **EIGHT**

FORTRESS.

It was late. Most of Project 17's agents were in their rooms, asleep or preparing for bed. The night-watch staff was in place. Colonel Hunter and Colonel Pearce of Citadel were walking together along a corridor.

"I didn't want to speak to you about this on the phone, Peter," said Colonel Pearce. "Just in case."

Colonel Hunter glanced at her sharply, but said nothing.

"McDermott is making noises to the Home Secretary and to our own superiors about having you replaced,"

Colonel Pearce continued in an undertone. "Did you know that?"

Colonel Hunter gave a slight shrug. "It doesn't surprise me," he said levelly. "I'm well aware of his opinions."

"But did you realize that the Director General is listening to him this time?" asked Colonel Pearce. "Questions are being asked about why you haven't yet issued the Codeword Rogue on Quicksilver."

"I'm not going to bring all that down on the boy just because he's been missing for a few hours," said Colonel Hunter. "I'm giving him until nine o'clock tomorrow morning. That's my deadline."

Colonel Pearce nodded thoughtfully. "Very well," she said. "If necessary, I'll speak up for you, and I know Philip Connolly is on your side, but Rampart is not a strong department, and you are even weaker now, Peter. You're still on the Director General's watch list following that incident earlier in the year with Agent Ballerina."

"I'm fully aware of that, Margaret," said Colonel Hunter crisply.

There was a brief pause.

"Do you think Quicksilver is a traitor?" Colonel Pearce asked at last.

"I'm quite certain he isn't," Colonel Hunter replied. "Although I still have no idea why he chose to absent himself in the way he did. I've had that tramp friend of his under close watch since it happened – the man known as Dodge. But I don't think he was involved. I've also made discreet enquiries at the children's home and they know nothing, I'm sure."

"My department is at your full disposal," said Colonel Pearce. "Citadel will do all it can to help you find the boy. We've been friends for a long time, Peter. You only have to ask."

"Thank you, Margaret," said Colonel Hunter. "You know that I've always valued your friendship and advice."

His Mob let out a soft sound like the croaking of a frog.

Frowning, the Colonel took it out, recognizing the ringtone.

"Yes, Bug? What is it?"

He knew Bug kept strange hours, but this was late even for him.

"I need to speak to you, Control," came Bug's wavering voice. "There's something really important I have to tell you."

"Meet me at my office in two minutes," said Colonel Hunter, breaking the line. He looked at Colonel Pearce. "Come with me, Margaret," he said, striding ahead. "I think we may be about to get some answers."

*

Bug stood waiting in the outer office. The lights were on and the computer was on standby, but the Colonel's secretary was gone. At this time of night the Graveyard Team, which was located in another office, would field all calls to Fortress.

He should never have left it this late to speak up. What had he been thinking? Switch was right: Silver could be in all kinds of danger. This had to be cleared up. Not that Switchblade had acted in a thought-through way when he'd found out what was happening. That was something else Bug had to explain to Control.

The door opened. Colonel Hunter and Colonel Pearce walked in. They barely glanced at Bug as they passed, but Colonel Hunter gestured for him to follow.

Colonel Hunter sat behind his desk, Colonel Pearce standing at his back, her arms folded and her face severe. Again without speaking, Colonel Hunter indicated with a flick of his hand that Bug should sit in the chair facing the desk.

Bug sat, quaking under the stern eyes of the two formidable Colonels.

"Don't be scared," Colonel Hunter said gently. "Tell us what you know."

Bug looked into his eyes.

Yes. It was time to tell him everything.

He just hoped he hadn't left it too late.

Creak.

Zak's eyes opened. For a moment or two he was disorientated. He was lying on his back on a narrow bed, fully clothed except for his shoes, staring up at the underside of another bed in a small wood-panelled room bathed in soft lamplight. The room vibrated to the rhythmic rumble of wheels on tracks. Rain streaked sideways along the window, like long silvery worms against the night sky.

What on earth . . . ?

Then his mind clicked in and it all made sense.

He was on the Orient-Express. He must have crashed out without undressing.

He turned his head, seeing a long thin slit of light from the doorway. Someone was opening the door to his cabin. Slowly. Stealthily. That was what had woken him.

Alarm bells rang in Zak's head and his sleepiness evaporated in an instant. A knot of fear tightened in his stomach. Stupid to be caught unprepared like this. What kind of an agent was he? He'd thought he'd be safe on the train. He'd jumped aboard at the very last moment. Anyone following him would have been left stranded on the platform.

But what if someone was already on the train?

All his senses were tingling now. He held his breath, watching intently as the door opened wider. A dark shape moved into the oblong of light coming from the corridor. Even in the half-light, with the upper bunk hiding the man's face, Zak could see that he was not wearing the stewards' blue uniform.

This was bad. Very bad.

Zak reached cautiously for his holdall, which was lying open beside the bed. His fingers closed around the hard cold metal of the gun.

He had been trained in how to disarm a person carrying a handgun, but agents were not taught how to fire weapons until they were several years older than Zak. All the same, the feel of the gun in his hand was reassuring, even if he had no real idea of how to use it.

You just point the thing and squeeze the trigger. How hard could it be?

Pretty hard when there's a live human being in front of you.

Zak sat up. "Put your hands in the air and stay right where you are," he said steadily, aiming the gun. He was glad that his voice hadn't revealed how scared he was feeling. The figure froze.

Zak got off the bed. The man had a heavy-set, deeply tanned face and sleek dark hair. His eyes were jet black under thick brows.

He was not one of the men from the Eiffel Tower.

"Shooting me would be a mistake," the man said in a thick Italian accent. "I am unarmed and I mean you no harm. I have information for you. Information about Archangel. He is not what you think. You would be unwise to trust him." The man moved a little further into the cabin, his hands still raised high. The door swung closed behind him.

Zak took a step backwards, the gun aimed at the man's chest.

"So, tell me," Zak said. "I'm listening."

"First, put down the gun, *giovane*, there's no need for you to threaten me." He smiled, edging closer. "I am *innocuo* – how you say? Harmless." His smile broadened. "Besides, you still have the safety catch on, so what use is the gun to you?"

Zak glanced at the gun. *The safety catch?*

The man lunged forwards, his smile gone. One large hand ripped the gun from Zak's grasp as the other reached for his throat.

Zak twisted away, colliding with the small side table. The lamp tottered and crashed and the room was plunged into darkness. Zak crouched low, his hands on the carpet, fingers spread, his legs bent under him. Gathering strength, he boosted himself upwards, his head thumping into the man's stomach.

The man gave a grunt and stumbled backwards, but his hand closed around the back of Zak's neck, his squeezing fingers making Zak gasp in pain. Zak laced his fingers together and delivered a two-fisted punch into the man's abdomen. The fingers loosened on his neck as the man doubled over.

Zak rammed his shoulder under the man's chin, lifting him upright again and sending him staggering across the small room. The man came to a halt against the door, gasping and shaking his head.

Zak eyed him, out of breath, his brain whirring. The only way to get to safety was through that door. But there was so little room in here. A plan formed in his mind. Leap for the upper bunk, grab hold of the edge and bring his legs round, using his momentum to kick the guy in the face. Harsh, but effective. With any luck, he'd go down like a felled tree.

The man glared as he lifted his hand.

Zak was aware of the gun a split second before he

saw the flash and heard the soft pop of the silenced shot. Something burned past Zak's ear as he flicked his head aside. There was a sharp splinter of sound as the bullet went through the window, leaving a small hole surrounded by a tracery of cracks.

He was never going to get past that gun.

Zak twisted around, bringing his hands down on the window catch. As the window swung open, cold air blasted into the cabin, flecked with rain.

Zak jumped, snatching at the top of the frame and dragging himself out. His feet hit the lower sill. He straightened his legs, his body outside the train now, buffeted by wind and rain. He reached for something to grip above the window.

His hands found a metal ridge. He curled his fingers around it and hauled his body upwards, the muscles of his shoulders and arms straining to their utmost. The roof was slippery with the rain, but Zak managed to swing a leg up and catch the ridge with his heel. A moment later, he was sprawled flat on his face on the roof of the train, clinging on as the rain lashed his skin and the wind tore at his clothes.

Now what? His escape through the window had been an instinctive reaction to being shot at. But he couldn't just lie here. Lightning forked across the sky and a fraction of a second later he heard a great shuddering roll of thunder.

In the brief flash of the lightning, Zak saw that the train was travelling through open countryside rimmed with mountains. He tried to wipe the rain from his eyes with one sleeve, but his clothes were already saturated, and the rain was relentless.

Still, he was safe for the moment – if you could call clinging to the roof of a speeding train in the middle of a thunderstorm *safe*. At least that freak with the gun couldn't get at him.

Suddenly, Zak felt a hand clasp hard around his ankle. The man was clambering up after him. Zak was not out of trouble yet.

Zak twisted onto his back and kicked at the hand. He heard a grunt of pain, but still the hand pulled him, dragging him across the slippery roof. If he were ripped from the roof while the train was going at this speed, the fall would probably kill him.

The man's rain-washed face appeared over the edge of the roof, his mouth stretched in a grimace of effort as his other hand snatched at the ridge.

Zak kicked again at the restraining hand and this time he managed to wrench his ankle free. He scooted backwards across the roof on his hands and heels, then managed to get shakily to his feet. He spread his legs, keeping low, feeling the swaying rhythm of the train under him, blinking the driving rain out of his eyes and trying to balance himself against the rush of the wind.

Doing this was hard enough without some murderous gangster chasing him down to kill him. And one thing was sure – the Italian gunman was very athletic. He was on the roof in a few moments, kneeling at first, catching his breath, then standing up, adjusting his stance to the movements of the carriage, reaching into his pocket for the gun, his eyes fixed on Zak, his stare deadly.

Zak turned and ran. He came to the end of the carriage and jumped. Lightning blinded him for a moment. He crashed down on his knees, the sound of thunder beating in his head. The fall saved him. He heard the whistle of a bullet as it skimmed above his head.

Then he was up again, running into the rain and wind, his half-closed eyes swimming with water so that it was difficult to see where he was going. But he could still feel the curve of the roof under his feet; still judge when he was in danger of sliding off.

He came to a second gap between carriages. He was running towards the engine. Was that a good plan? The whine of another bullet burned in his ear. The shudder and roll of the train was making it hard for the man to aim, but he only needed to get lucky once.

The noise of the bullet drove a new plan into Zak's head. The carriages were linked by flexible collars of rubber and steel. He faked a stumble, crying out and falling down between the carriages as though the bullet had hit him. He landed safely, sprawling flat on the corrugated top and preparing himself for what was coming. He rose to a crouch, pressing in under the roof of the trailing carriage, counting the micro-seconds.

Sure enough, the man came to the edge of the carriage, looming over Zak, his clothes shedding water, his legs spread for balance. Zak lunged upwards, grabbing at the man's legs with both arms and pulling with all his strength. The man toppled over and crashed onto his back. Zak saw the gun jolt out of his fingers. It bounced along the roof, and then slid over the edge into the rain-filled darkness.

Zak sprang back onto the roof, trying to remember his martial arts training. He had been taught some wickedly effective Krav Maga techniques – kicks and punches designed to go for the most vulnerable parts of an opponent's body in order to disable him and bring the fight to a swift end. It was one thing to try them out in training, but Zak hesitated at the idea of stomping down with all his strength on a man's knee in order to snap his leg. Too brutal. Too vicious.

Instead, he jumped over the man, using the buffeting wind to add to his momentum. The man's fingers clawed at him but missed, and he landed sure-footedly and raced away along the carriage roof, kicking up spumes of rainwater as he went.

He glanced back and saw that the man was on his feet again and running after him, spread-legged for balance. He was hunched low and now carried a knife in his fist.

Zak gave a grim smile. *You think you're going to catch me? Think again, loser.* He was almost back at the place where he had climbed out of the window. All he needed do was to slide down the side of the carriage, boost himself in through the window and slam it shut behind him.

Job done.

He timed his moves perfectly, edging to the rim of the roof, dropping to his knees, skidding a little on the wet metal – but keeping under control. He grasped the ridge with both hands and swung down. His feet bounced off the closed window, jarring his legs, almost jerking his fingers loose. He twisted his head, trying to see what had happened.

The force of the wind had blown the window closed. There was no way back into the train from here. He hung for a few moments, wondering what to do next. His arms were stretched above his head, his knees bent up against his chest, his feet on the closed window. The rain smacked into his face and the wind tried to rip him from the side of the carriage. A flash of lightning illuminated the countryside, turning it all into stark black and white, bleaching the rain to silver spears.

His only option was to get back onto the roof and try to find some other way into the train. He tensed then released the muscles in his legs, so that his feet pushed him up again. But those precious wasted seconds had allowed his pursuer to get alarmingly close.

Zak sprinted towards the back of the train. He had no real plan now, except to keep clear of that guy's knife. He leaped from carriage to carriage, looking behind every now and then, glad to see that the man was falling back.

Then he ran out of train.

He stood teetering on the brink of the final carriage. He could jump and trust to his luck. But even if he landed safely, he would be in the middle of nowhere.

He turned, the rain pounding on his face. The man was coming closer. Zak took a long deep breath and prepared himself to fight. No more hesitation, no more unease. When the man came within reach, Zak would have to call on his martial arts training. His only other option would be a knife in the ribs.

The man slowed, his dark eyes burning. The knife glimmered in his fist.

As Zak watched the man approach, he heard the voice of his trainer in his head. *Time your strike. Control your breath. Aim for a spot ten to fifteen centimetres behind your opponent so you deliver your blow with maximum impact.*

The man loomed closer, huge and dark and deadly. The knife had a serrated edge. A hunting knife, Zak guessed. A long, razor-sharp hunting knife.

It was time for Zak to fight for his life.

Suddenly the train slowed, the carriages shuddering and rocking violently. The sound of metal grinding on metal shrieked above the howl of the wind and the rattle of the rain.

The train screeched to a halt, and the carriage rolled under Zak's feet. He was sent stumbling forwards. He cannoned into the man and the two of them lost their footing and slid over the edge of the carriage into the darkness.

CHAPTER **NINE**

FORTRESS.
04.46
BUG'S OFFICE.

Bug would have preferred it if Colonel Hunter had yelled at him. But Control had not lost his temper, even when Bug had told him everything he knew about Quicksilver's disappearance, and followed that up by informing him that Switchblade had also gone rogue. Switch was out there now, alone and without authorization, chasing after Quicksilver.

Switch had waited only long enough to get a solid lead on Quicksilver's location, then he'd gone. No waiting for permission, no word to anyone else – he had simply dropped his Mob into Bug's lap and vanished.

No Mob meant no way of contacting him. No way for Control to call him and reel him in. Not that Bug was in any doubt as to where Switch was heading. He was on his way to stop Quicksilver and convince him to return to Fortress voluntarily.

Bug brought up the same screen that he had shown Switchblade – a satellite map of Europe. The map was sliding slowly down the screen, north to south. A red spot pulsed rhythmically in the centre. A red dot that followed a railway line.

Colonel Hunter stood behind Bug's chair, watching the dot on the map, speaking in rapid and fluent French into his own Mob.

Bug avoided eye contact with the Colonel. He was feeling bad. He couldn't decide who he'd let down worse in all this mess. Quicksilver, Switchblade or the Colonel. He had the horrible feeling he'd failed them all.

Colonel Hunter finished his call to the *Direction Centrale du Renseignement Intérieur*, the French Secret Services Directorate, but before he could speak to Bug, another call came in. It was from William Kent of the

MI5 Director General's office. It was obvious that a lot of people had been ordered out of bed early this morning. Fortress's troubles were creating ever-widening ripples through the British Secret Services.

"Yes, Mr Kent, that's correct," the Colonel said. "Two agents have now left Fortress without my explicit permission. No, the Director General need not be alarmed. I have the situation under complete control. I know where they both are, and I fully expect them to be picked up within the hour by a team from the DCRI in France."

Bug pressed a key and the satellite image zoomed in closer, night-vision technology lighting up the screen in eerie shades of green as the camera followed the train through open countryside.

"Quicksilver is on a train," said the Colonel. "Switchblade may already be with him, and if not, he will certainly be somewhere close by. I have alerted the Central Directorate of Interior Intelligence in Paris and they intend to stop the train as soon as possible. Quicksilver will be apprehended and brought back to Fortress." There was a pause. "Yes, Mr Kent, you can tell the Director General that I will call him the moment I have confirmation that Quicksilver is in custody."

He ended the call and pocketed his Mob. He leaned

on the back of Bug's chair, his eyes on the screen. The image slowed and came to a stop.

"Got him!" Colonel Hunter murmured under his breath. "You had better have a good explanation for your actions, Quicksilver. If not, there's nothing I can do to save you."

Years of tricky and acrobatic free running had taught Zak how to take a fall. He curled into a ball as he hit the ground, knees to his chest, arms up to protect his head as he rolled and bounced down a steep earthen embankment.

He came to a sprawling halt in a waterlogged ditch. Spitting out muddy water, Zak staggered to his feet. His hair was plastered over his eyes and the world spun around him like a top. He waded out of the ditch and climbed onto drier land. The train loomed above him, almost black against the sky. A few yellow lights glimmered and, as he stared up, he saw more lights coming on along the length of the train as rudely awoken passengers began to emerge from under their duvets, wondering what had happened.

Zak gazed into the darkness under the embankment, expecting to see the knife-man lying somewhere close by. *With his neck broken, with any luck,* Zak thought, only half-kidding. He didn't want the man dead – he wanted him awake and tied up and spilling his guts. Who was he? Who had sent him? How had he found Gabriel? How did he know Zak was involved?

Some instinct made Zak turn. The man was right behind him, alive, upright and still wielding his knife. Zak ducked as his knife arm came down, slicing the air where Zak's neck had been a moment before.

Zak dived aside as the man wheeled and aimed another blow at him, thrusting upwards this time, meaning to catch him in the stomach. There was blood on the man's face – he had obviously hit something sharp on the way down – but there was also a look of absolute determination in his eyes. He was here to kill Zak, and nothing was going to stop him.

Except that Zak had no intention of being killed.

Zak's feet skidded on the wet grass as he flung himself past the man and sped away into the darkness. He heard the man yell something as he turned and chased after him.

Lightning turned the world to black and white. The distant mountains stood out stark and sharp against the dark rain-filled sky. Across a wide field, Zak saw a huddle of trees. A good place to play hide and seek. He focused on the deep gloom under the trees as he picked up speed.

He sprinted across the field and plunged into the trees. Sliding into cover behind one of the trunks, he glanced back. The man was running towards him. He was fast, but he wasn't fast enough. Not by a long way.

Zak moved deeper into the darkness, jogging now, looking over his shoulder. The man was following him, prowling through the trunks, the knife glittering faintly in his fist.

Zak snatched a stone and shoved it into the front of his T-shirt. Then he bent his knees and jumped, grabbing a low branch and dragging himself up onto it. He climbed higher, then became still, his heart beating fast as he peered down through the leaves.

He saw the man move under the tree and then pause, his head turning this way and that, trying to work out which way his quarry had gone.

Try looking up, dimbo.

Doing his utmost to avoid shaking the branch he was squatting on, Zak pulled the rock from underneath his T-shirt. He held his breath as he brought his arm back, then flung the stone as hard as he could.

It went sailing through the branches, landing with a clearly audible thump some way off. The man's body went rigid for a moment, his head snapping around in the direction from which the sound had come. Then he pushed forwards and disappeared beneath the branches.

Zak climbed down the tree and dropped to the ground.

Sucker!

Moving stealthily, Zak headed back the way he had come. The guy could spend the rest of the night searching the forest – Zak was going straight to the train. Once he was on board he'd be safe.

He peered through the teeming rain. There were even more lights on the train now. Across the stormy darkness, it looked like a warm, comfortable place to be.

And then, to his deep alarm, he saw the train begin to move. Slowly at first, it started to crawl across the horizon, its lights blurred by the rain.

The train was leaving.

Oh no you don't!

Zak ran, his arms pumping hard at his sides. He saw something speed past his shoulder and embed itself in the grass in front of him.

A knife!

He glanced back. The man was coming for him at full speed, shouting, his feet kicking up fountains of water. Not so dumb after all. And fast – very fast.

Zak raced past the knife, not daring to pause and pick it up. The train was gathering speed, sliding away on the high embankment.

Another quick look back. The man had stooped on the run and snatched up the knife again.

Focus, Zak! Get with it!

Zak fixed his sight on the train, his mind and body meshing as his feet skimmed the grass. In the zone.

He was close now. Only a few metres away. He pounded up the embankment, his arm already reaching for the train.

But it was getting faster by the moment, drawing away from him. Not even *he* could outrun a train.

He was on the tracks now, running like he had never run in his life. Still the train was moving away. A few precious seconds and it would be out of reach. He'd be stranded there with the rain and the lightning and the knife-man.

Panic put him into some kind of overdrive. The world around him blurred, the rain hitting him like shrapnel, his legs rising and falling like machine pistons. He leaned forwards, reaching out frantically with stretched fingers and straining muscles.

But still he couldn't reach.

Suddenly a door at the back of the train swung open

and a hand reached towards him. Fingers closed around his wrist, pulling him forwards. His feet slithered from under him but the hand didn't let him fall. He was hauled up onto the train and sent sliding along the floor, gasping and thrashing like a stranded fish.

The door closed with a snap, shutting out the noise of the storm. Zak was shoved onto his back, his eyes swimming.

"End of the line, Quicksilver!" said a voice.

FORTRESS.

"Yes, Mr Kent, the train has been stopped," Colonel Hunter said into his Mob. He looked at Bug, placing his finger over the Mob's mike. "Any word from the DCRI team?" he asked.

Bug shook his head. "Nothing so far." He could hear voices over his headset. It was tuned to the frequency of the French security force that was sweeping the train. The agreed codewords for when they found and apprehended Quicksilver were Fish Landed. In the event of something going wrong they were to report: Flying Fish.

The men aboard the train were talking rapidly among

themselves, although none had said the words to show that Zak was in custody. But the tracker bug was giving out a strong steady signal. It could only be a matter of moments now.

Two men in dark suits moved rapidly along the train corridor. One of them held a small electronic device with a blue-lit screen. A red dot pulsed a little way from the crosshairs on the grid.

Quicksilver was close. They almost had him.

They came to the closed door of a sleeping cabin. The red dot hit the cross hairs. They looked at one another and the lead man nodded.

They shoved the door open. A middle-aged man with a balding head and bleary eyes stared at them from the bottom bunk of the cabin, one hand reaching for his glasses.

"What's going on?" he croaked in a frightened voice.

The lead man pushed into the cabin and snatched up the Project 17 Flash that lay on the side table. "*Êtes-vous Anglais?*" barked the man.

"Yes, I am," said the man, shoving his glasses on his face. "My name is Bernard Johnson. I'm a salesman. I'm on my way to Essen for a conference."

"Where did you get this?" asked the French security officer, holding up the Flash.

The man blinked at him. "I . . . I found it," he stammered. "At the Eiffel Tower . . . it was just lying on the floor . . ."

The French agent drew a mobile phone out of his pocket and took a picture of the alarmed salesman. With a couple of touches to the screen, he emailed the picture to Fortress.

He turned and shook his head at his companion. "Flying Fish," he said into his Bluetooth. "*Je répète*: Flying Fish."

FORTRESS.

A picture flashed up on one of Bug's screens. It showed a round-faced man in spectacles, sitting up in a narrow bunk bed in navy-blue pyjamas and looking flustered and frightened.

A second picture showed a hand holding Quicksilver's Flash.

The codewords had come through a few moments earlier.

Flying Fish.

"Thank you," Colonel Hunter said into his Mob, speaking

now to the leader of the French security team on the train. "That's not him. You can let the train continue."

He turned to the satellite image. "Overlay a map, please, Bug," he asked wearily. Bug hit keys and a map appeared, revealing that the train had been halted just before the French border with Germany.

Colonel Hunter gazed silently at the map for a few moments.

"Where was the tracking signal when Switchblade took off?" he asked.

"Heading for Paris," Bug replied, well aware of how badly the disappointment of the aborted mission must have hit the Colonel. "On a line that terminated at the Gare de l'Est railway station." He looked up at the Colonel. "I don't know what could have happened."

"Quicksilver lost the Flash device when he was on the Eiffel Tower, it seems," said the Colonel. "But why was he there, and how did he come to lose it?"

Bug stared at him in silence. And where was Switch right now?

Colonel Hunter's Mob rang. "Yes, Lieutenant Colonel," he said, already walking to the door, his voice tight and strained. It must be Lieutenant Colonel McDermott of Bastion. Not one of Control's greatest pals. "No, they have not been apprehended yet. Yes, I will be contacting the Director General . . ." The Colonel pushed through the door of Bug's office and stalked down the corridor, his voice fading away as the door closed again.

Bug leaned back in his chair, puffing out his cheeks.

Things were not going well.

Zak blinked the rainwater out of his eyes and found himself staring up into Switchblade's face. His legs felt strange and rubbery and his shoulder was throbbing with pain from him being hauled onto the train.

Switch was sitting on the floor at his side, watching him with a stony, unreadable expression on his face.

Zak eyed him uneasily. Did this mean Colonel Hunter had managed to track him down? Was Switchblade here to drag him back to Fortress? Had word of his mission got around the Underground – around MI5? Did the mole already know all about it? That would be a disaster.

"How did you find me?" gasped Zak, pulling himself up so that he was leaning against the wall of the corridor. He winced, holding his aching shoulder.

"Hurt much?" Switch asked.

Zak nodded.

"Good," said Switch. "I should have ripped it right out and beaten you to death with it." His eyes were hard.

"What are you playing at, Silver? Have you any idea of the trouble you're in right now?"

"I can't go back, Switch,' said Zak. "I have to finish this." How much did Switch know? Would he be prepared to hear Zak out?

"Listen," Switch got to his feet, offering Zak a hand. "I'm a stowaway on board – but I'm guessing you have a cabin. Let's go there and talk."

There were a few stewards here and there as they walked along the train, but now the Orient Express was on the move again, things were starting to settle down. Zak and Switch made their way to the cabin without being seen.

Switch eyed the broken lamp and the bullet hole in the window.

Zak closed the door firmly and switched on the overhead light. "So, how did Colonel Hunter know how to find me?" he asked, going to the small cupboard and fishing out a towel to dry himself.

"Colonel Hunter doesn't know – at least, he didn't when I skipped out," said Switch. "I got here on my own."

Zak stared at him. The Colonel *hadn't* sent him?

"Bug put a tracker on you," Switch told him, sitting on the lower bunk. "He showed me a satellite map. It was obvious you were on a train heading for Paris. I made a unilateral decision to come and get you."

"Where's the tracker?" demanded Zak. "We have to get rid of it."

"It's in the Flash he gave you," Switch replied.

Zak gave a gasp of relief. "I lost it," he said.

Switch frowned. "When?"

"I was on the Eiffel Tower. There was a problem. It got knocked out of my hand. I didn't have time to pick it up."

Switch's eyes widened. "Then it's lucky you still had it on you last time I looked at the map," he said. "As soon as we worked out that the train you were on was heading for the Gare de l'Est in Paris I grabbed a few things and set off to find you before you got yourself into even worse trouble."

Zak stared at him. "You got all the way to Paris that quickly?" he asked.

Switch nodded. "I went to London City airport and took the first flight to Orly airport in Paris," he said. "I got there early evening yesterday. I went to the railway station and worked out you must have been on the Orient-Express. That was the only train that made sense, from what I'd seen on the satellite image. I sneaked on board, pretending to be one of the cleaners. It didn't take long for me to realize you weren't on the train, so I kept out of sight and waited." He gave a grim smile.

"There was a tricky moment when the train was about to get moving and there was still no sign of you. I began to think I'd got it wrong. I was about to get off when I saw you racing up the platform."

"Why didn't you let me know you were on board?" asked Zak, digging in his holdall for some dry clothes.

"I decided to hold off showing myself until I had a better idea of what you were up to," Switch replied. "I wanted to find out if you were with anyone."

"I should have been," said Zak. "But things got tricky."

"You can say that again," said Switch. "I waited till most people were in bed before I came to have a word with you. I saw a suspicious-looking guy creeping from cabin to cabin, opening the doors, looking in, then moving onto the next one."

"He had a gun," said Zak. "He was going to kill me."

Switch nodded. "I wondered at first whether he was someone you'd arranged to meet, but when I heard the punch-up going on in your cabin I realized something screwy was happening. By the time I got into the cabin, the pair of you had gone out of the window. I wasn't about to follow you, so I went to the end of the carriage and pressed the emergency button to stop the train."

"We were on the roof," said Zak. "When the train stopped, we fell off. I led him into some trees."

"I thought it must have been something like that," said Switch. "While the stewards were dealing with the complaining passengers, I slipped off and ran back down the track. I thought I'd find you lying there with your neck broken. But there was no sign of you, so I got back on the train. Then they started the train again and I didn't know whether to jump off or stay aboard or what." He smiled. "That's when I saw you, haring along the tracks behind us. That was quite a run, Silver – even for you."

"I didn't want to be stranded with the loony knife-man," said Zak.

The smile vanished from Switch's face. "Now I need you to tell me exactly what you're playing at, Silver," he said. "And, trust me, it had better be good."

Zak looked at Switch. He had come here to help him, without orders and without permission . . . the way a true friend would. He deserved to be told the whole story. Slowly and carefully, Zak did his best to explain to Switch everything that had happened since he had opened that package in Jubilee Gardens. The story wound down to the late-night attack by the Italian gunman. Zak became silent, watching Switch closely, wondering what he was thinking.

"Having that photo of your family and knowing

Slingshot's passwords doesn't mean Gabriel, or Archangel, or whatever he's called, is right about the mole," Switch said after a few moments of heavy silence. "Did he give you any evidence at all?"

Zak sighed. "No," he said. "That's the problem. He needs me to help him get the evidence."

"It's a bit like the chicken and the egg, isn't it?" said Switch. "Which comes first – the trust or the proof? Without proof, why trust him? Without trust, how do you get the proof?" He looked sharply at Zak. "*Do* you trust him?"

"Yes," Zak replied without hesitation. "Those two Italian men at the Eiffel Tower were hunting him down for sure. And the guy on the train was Italian too. That wasn't a coincidence. I think they're all part of the same gang. And they're killers, Switch. My guess is that Padrone sent them to find Gabriel and finish him off before he can unmask the mole. He's genuine, Switch, I'm certain of it . . . and I want to help him."

Switch frowned, taking this in. "I came here to try to talk you into going back to Fortress," he said.

"That's not going to happen," Zak said. "Not unless you tie me up and carry me back."

"How do you know *I'm* not the mole?" Switch asked suddenly.

"No offence," said Zak with the ghost of a smile. "But Gabriel said it was someone really important. Someone high up – as high as the Colonel, or even higher maybe."

Switch's eyes narrowed. "That's not good," he murmured. "That is *so* not good." His eyes flashed. "Okay, I'm with you, Silver." He glanced out of the window. "It'll be dawn soon, but we should get some sleep." He stood up. "Top bunk!" he declared, pulling himself up and stretching out.

Weary and sore, Zak lay on the bottom bunk. Switch was with him! He felt a huge sense of relief that he wasn't working alone any more. If anyone was capable of helping him see this through to the end, it was Switchblade.

"No snoring," ordered Switch, wrapping the covers around himself. "And you'd better hope your pal Gabriel comes up with the goods in Venice, or we're both for the chop. Control is not a happy bunny right now. Not a happy bunny at all."

CHAPTER **TEN**

THE HOME OFFICE, WESTMINSTER, LONDON.

The office was dominated by a long black table surrounded by high-backed chairs. A small group of people was gathered; one of them was speaking.

"This is an Inter-Departmental Ministerial Briefing, set up to discuss the situation in Project 17 arising from the unauthorized actions of two of its agents," he said. "People in attendance: Major Philip Connolly, Director of Rampart; Colonel Margaret Pearce, Director of Citadel;

Colonel Peter Hunter, Director of Fortress; Lieutenant Colonel Hector McDermott, Director of Bastion, and myself, John Mallin, in the Chair, representing the Home Secretary."

He turned to Colonel Hunter. "Am I correct in saying that you now have two rogue agents, Colonel?" he asked.

"Agent Switchblade is not rogue," Colonel Hunter said calmly, although the stiff posture of his body and the rapid pulse at his temple told a different story. "He simply anticipated my orders, and went in search of Quicksilver. The two incidents are quite different."

"So you are in contact with Switchblade, are you?" asked Lieutenant Colonel McDermott. "He's acting under your orders?"

"He is not acting in contravention to any direct orders," Colonel Hunter replied guardedly, holding his temper in check with some difficulty. "He is in the field, seeking to locate Quicksilver."

"And do you have any further information to explain Quicksilver's actions?" asked Mr Mallin.

"Nothing new," said Colonel Hunter. He had been careful in his report not to lay any blame on Bug, and he wasn't about to change that now. "Quicksilver received an unknown message and left Fortress without permission. We believe he is in Europe. We have no

reason to assume he is involved in anything criminal or contrary to the interests of the United Kingdom."

"The boy has gone off on some wild-goose chase of his own," interrupted Lieutenant Colonel McDermott gruffly. "What else would you expect from a fourteen-year-old boy taken off the streets like that?"

"He was not taken off the streets, Lieutenant Colonel," said Colonel Pearce. "He was in residential council care. From what I have seen, he is an intelligent, reliable and trustworthy agent."

"With a criminal record," Lieutenant Colonel McDermott replied.

"He was involved in a few minor scrapes with the police," admitted Colonel Hunter. "But the most recent of those was almost three years ago."

"All the same," said Major Connolly, "he's only been in Project 17 for a few months. Are you entirely sure you can trust him?"

"Yes, *entirely*," Colonel Hunter said firmly. "Quicksilver appears to have acted rashly and without due consideration for the consequences of his behaviour, but I have no reason to assume he has sinister intentions." He could see where this was going. Margaret Pearce was on his side, but Connolly was wavering and McDermott was against him. "And I would like to add that I think

this meeting is being held at an inappropriate time."
He stood up. "I have more important things to do than
justify my leadership of Project 17." He nodded to John
Mallin. "If you will excuse me."

He marched to the door and closed it quietly but firmly
behind him. He stalked down the corridor, well aware that
the meeting would continue without him. McDermott
would be calling for him to be removed from control of
Fortress. Margaret Pearce would be in his corner but, if
Connolly followed McDermott, things would get difficult.
And if Mallin turned against him, then the Home Secretary
would very likely relieve him of command.

He strode across the foyer and out into the street. Zak
Archer going rogue had put him and the whole future
of Project 17 under immense pressure. If Quicksilver
wasn't found quickly, the whole unit could be taken out
of his hands or, worse yet, closed down entirely.

The stakes could not be higher.

Zak had breakfast alone in the dining car, tucking away
a few edibles to take back for Switch. A strange face at
Zak's table would not have been easy to explain away,
especially as Switch was on board the Orient-Express
without a ticket. During Zak's absence, the steward

restored his cabin to its daytime state, while Switch slipped off to the luggage wagon to wait him out.

Zak managed to disguise the bullet hole in the window by leaning his bag up against it. Fortunately, the steward didn't move it or there would have been some awkward questions.

When Zak got back from breakfast, the bunks had been converted back into a sofa and the steward was just heading off with the bed linen. Zak apologized for the broken table lamp.

"Bad dream," he explained to the steward. "I thrashed about a bit." He performed some crazy octopus-like swings with his arms. "I'm always breaking stuff at home."

"Not a problem, Mr Taylor," the steward told him. "These things happen."

"So, what was all that last night with the sudden stop?" Zak asked, trying to sound innocent. "It woke me up."

"No one is quite sure," said the steward. "Either it was a prank by some mischievous passenger – pressing the emergency button for a joke – or it was some kind of malfunction." He plumped up the cushions on the restored sofa. "It's nothing to worry about, Mr Taylor. We'll easily pick up the lost time."

Switch slid in soon after the steward had left.

The train halted at Innsbruck for a brief time. Beyond

the railway station, the Alps rose in steep green folds, their peaks capped with snow that shone pale blue in the sunlight. The heavy storm clouds had vanished and the sky was clear and bright.

"Something's been worrying me," Zak said. They were sitting in the cabin watching the city of Innsbruck shrink into the distance as the train pulled away. "How did that guy from last night know I was Gabriel's contact? Apart from me and Gabriel, no one else was supposed to know I was involved."

Switch frowned. "That's a good question," he said. "You and Gabriel have never met, right?"

"Not even close," agreed Zak. "And Gabriel said the phones we've been talking on are pretty much untraceable."

Switch snapped his fingers. "Got it," he said. "It must have been Bug's tracker. Padrone's people must have known Gabriel would make contact with a British agent. They must have been scanning for anyone using British Secret Service frequencies – so when they picked up the signal from Bug's tracker they moved in on it. If there is a mole high up in the Service, he could easily have passed on all the usual frequency bands to Padrone." Switch nodded. "That's how they found you on the Eiffel Tower. And those two guys who grabbed you there could have

taken a mobile phone picture of you and mailed it to all their mates."

"Including one who was lurking on the train," said Zak. "Thanks, Bug, for almost getting me killed."

"He was worried about you," said Switch.

"I know," said Zak. "I don't really blame him." He took the phone out of his pocket. "I wish Gabriel would call!"

Zak laid the mobile phone on the side table. He was keeping it on permanently now, despite his concerns about running down the battery.

Switch leaned forwards on the sofa with his chin in his hands, staring intently at the phone as though he hoped to make it ring by willpower alone.

"I'll tell you one thing," he said. "If my take on how they found you is right, it makes Gabriel's story about a high-up mole in the Secret Service a lot more likely to be correct." He looked at Zak. "But it also means Gabriel could have sold you out."

"Why would he do that?"

"He might have put them onto you in order to get them off his own back," said Switch.

"He wouldn't do that," said Zak.

"Are you one hundred per cent sure?" Switch asked quietly.

"Yes." But was he? Really? *One hundred per cent?*

Gabriel had made it quite clear that he was determined to complete the mission, no matter what the odds. Would he betray Zak in order to escape the Italians? Was it entirely impossible? After all, how much did he really know about Gabriel? A voice on the phone. A man who had once worked with Jason. Was Zak being *too* trusting?

The Orient-Express rumbled on.

The countryside rolled by.

Time passed. Very . . . slowly . . .

"What if he never calls?" Zak wondered aloud as the train swept through lush green countryside with stark mountains rearing up on either side. The brochure informed them that they were passing through the Italian Dolomites. The scenery was spectacular, but the inactivity was driving the two of them mad. "What if we get to Venice and he isn't there?"

Switch gave him a sidelong glance. "You're starting with the 'what ifs' *now*?" he said. "You told me you trusted him."

"I do," said Zak. "I meant, what if *they've* got to him? What if he's – you know – dead or something?"

"He's not dead," said Switch. "He'll call."

"Why are you so sure?"

"Because if he doesn't, I'm going to strangle you for getting me into this," Switch said with dark humour, his eyes returning to the phone on the table. "First, I'm going to kill you stone dead, then, when I get to Venice, I'm going to enrol in a gondoliering class. I'll need a new career path, because there's no way Control will ever let me back into Project 17 after this."

"You got *yourself* into this," Zak said, very nearly smiling. "Don't blame me." He was glad Switch was here with him. Nothing seemed impossible when Switchblade was around. Gabriel would ring. He'd explain everything. Life would make sense again.

Switch snorted but didn't respond.

"How do you think he'll get to Venice?" Zak asked after a while.

"Aeroplane from Paris to the Marco Polo airport in Venice, then a taxi to Santa Lucia station, where we'll be pulling in," said Switch. "He could be there already if he got his skates on."

Zak leaned forwards. "What if there are more of those Italian guys on the train?" he asked. "Should we maybe barricade ourselves in here?"

"I think they'd have made themselves known by now," said Switch. "I'm pretty sure the one you left back in the thunderstorm was working alone. But you're right,

we need to keep our eyes peeled. He's bound to have called his boss to say you're still alive and heading for Venice." He threw out his arm, one commanding finger pointing at the phone. "Ring!" he demanded.

Nothing happened.

"Does that ever work?" Zak asked with a small grin.

"It was worth a shot," said Switch, throwing himself back into the sofa and folding his arms. Zak had the feeling Switchblade was going a little stir-crazy, cooped up in the small cabin all day with nothing to do and nowhere to go. Zak felt the same. The amazing mountain scenery was fine, but he'd rather be running through it than watching it from a train window.

The phone rang almost before Switch's head hit the cushion.

Zak snatched it up.

"Gabriel?"

"Zak, you're safe," came the familiar voice.

"Just about," Zak replied, relief flooding through him. "You?"

"I've just arrived at Marco Polo airport," said Gabriel. "I don't think I've been followed."

"You might not have been, but I have!" said Zak. "There was a guy on the train. He tried to kill me. With a gun."

"What happened?" Gabriel sounded alarmed.

"He fell off the roof and . . ." Zak checked himself. "I'll explain later. We had a tussle. He lost. I won. I'm fine, but they know what I look like." He glanced at Switch, wondering whether to tell Gabriel that he was with another Project 17 agent. For some reason – maybe because he was worried it would freak Gabriel out – he decided not to. "What happens now?" he asked.

"Padrone's people are on high alert," said Gabriel. "My cover's obviously been completely blown, but so far they haven't managed to get to me." There was a pause. "There's no way we can meet at the railway station. Use Foxhunt Rules to get out of the station without being followed," he said. "Once you're certain you're not being tracked, make your way to the Fondamente Nove. Plenty of people speak English, so you shouldn't have too much trouble finding it. Take a waterbus from Fondamente Nove to the island of Burano – they run every half an hour. Then take the boat to another island, Torcello. I'll meet you there in the ruins of the palazzo."

"Got it," said Zak.

"Don't lead them to me, Zak," said Gabriel. "Be vigilant, okay?" He lowered his voice. "Or we're both dead."

Zak put the phone down. Gabriel's final words sent a shiver down his spine.

"You didn't mention me," said Switch.

"I didn't want to have to explain how you found me," Zak said. "He'd have got spooked."

Switch nodded. "I'll keep a low profile," he said. "How long till we hit Venice?"

Zak glanced at his watch then checked the travel brochure. "Two and a half hours," he said. "We're due in at Santa Lucia station at five o'clock."

"Good," said Switch, stretching out on the sofa and closing his eyes. "Wake me up when we get there."

Zak looked at him in surprise.

Zak was so wired he was almost bouncing off the walls – and Switch was going to take a *nap*?

How cool was that?

The Orient-Express slowed as it made its way across the bridge that spanned the wide waters of Venice's Grand Canal. It glided to a halt in the terminus of Santa Lucia station. Gazing out of the window, Zak was quite surprised by how modern the station looked. He'd always thought of Venice as a really old city of elaborate, crumbling buildings crammed together on either side of narrow canals. But this place was all steel and concrete and glass.

"How do you want to play this?" asked Switch. Zak had only woken him five minutes ago, but Switch was already fully alert. "We have to assume there are people waiting for you here – people who most likely know exactly what you look like."

Zak was surprised that Switch hadn't taken control of the situation. Switch gave a grim smile as he saw the confusion in Zak's eyes.

"Hey, this is *your* mission," he said. "I'll help in any way I can, but you're running things. I trust you, Silver. You can do this."

Zak thought quickly. The train had stopped and the doors had been flung open. The first few passengers were already stepping onto the platform and heading for the exit, carrying bags or pulling wheeled suitcases along behind them. There was an excited buzz in the air.

He peered up and down the platform, searching for anything suspicious. But how would he know? If Padrone's people were here, they could look like anyone – a porter, some guy sitting reading a newspaper. Even a couple strolling arm in arm across the concourse could be hiding bad intentions.

"I'm going to get out on the side away from the platform," Zak said at last. "I'll cross the tracks, get up onto

the other platform and leg it out of here at top speed."

Switch nodded. "Where shall we meet?"

"Gabriel told me to get a waterbus from a place called Fondamente Nove and meet up with him in the ruins of the palazzo on the island of Torcello," said Zak. "We can meet up at the place where the waterbuses are moored. Gabriel said to use Foxhunt Rules."

Switch nodded. "Good plan. But don't get lost, Venice is a big place." He gave Zak a quick smile. "And be careful – apparently the streets are full of water."

"No problem," said Zak. "I'm a good swimmer."

They stood looking at one another for a few moments, then Zak picked up his holdall and opened the cabin door. He waited while people passed him in the corridor, talking animatedly, lugging bags, trying to keep children under control.

At last, the corridor was empty. Glancing back at Switch one final time, Zak slipped out, padded to the nearest door, opened it and dropped down to the tracks. Clutching the holdall under his arm, he darted across then launched himself up onto the far platform.

A few people stopped, staring at him. A man in uniform shouted something in Italian and ran towards him. But Zak was off. He sprinted down the platform, dodging and weaving through the people until he came

to the exit. He ducked as another uniformed man tried to grab him.

He raced at top speed across a wide concourse, vaguely aware of souvenir shops and news stands and snack bars. The concourse opened on to a flight of steps that led down to a paved square and the greeny-blue water of the Grand Canal. The briny smell of salt water struck him and took him by surprise – he knew Venice was surrounded by water and threaded with canals, but for some reason he had not expected it to smell like a seaside town.

A low grey building stood by the water's edge. A large, square boat was moored close by. He remembered information from the Invitation to Board brochure. The vaporetto waterbuses were the best way for tourists to get around.

The grey building was the ticket office. He dived inside and joined a queue of people waiting to buy tickets. He was watchful, alert to every movement around him, his nerves stretched to their limits.

There was ticket information in several languages. He got to the front of the queue and bought a tourist travel card. While waiting, he'd been studying a wall map of the waterways, illustrated throughout with images of major tourist attractions.

"Could you tell me how I get to the Basilica di San Marco, please?" he asked, choosing a tourist attraction at random.

He listened to the instructions, nodding and smiling.

"*Grazie*," he said, using up his full store of Italian in one go. "Thanks."

He left the ticket booth and got onto the crowded waterbus. The Basilica was an amazing old church that dated back almost a thousand years – but he had no intention of going there. If anyone *had* managed to follow him from the railway station, he hoped they would have overheard his question. That way, Padrone's gang would be closing in on San Marco while Zak was heading in an entirely different direction.

Foxhunt Rules.

He kept close to the gangplank as the waterbus filled up. Watching without being too conspicuous. Waiting for the last moment.

Just as the gangplank was about to be drawn away, he jumped off the boat and ran. He flicked a look over his shoulder. No one was following. Still, there was no reason to feel pleased with himself – not just yet. Padrone's people knew what he looked like – he'd have to be on his toes every second he was here. Foxhunt Rules all the way.

CHAPTER **ELEVEN**

It was an astonishing and bewildering journey for Zak as he made his way across the ancient city to the Fondamente Nove. He decided not to ask directions from anyone he encountered on the streets. Instead, he dived into small shops and tried to make himself understood to people behind the counters. Most spoke some form of broken English, and soon he was running through narrow, twisting streets full of decaying old buildings, crowded with tourists and bustling with small hotels and gift shops and restaurants.

The sheer number of people on the streets was a plus

and a minus. The good thing about it was that he could duck and dodge in among them and feel as though he was hiding in the crowd. The bad part was that it was impossible to tell if he was being followed.

He found the Ponte delle Guglie – a small stone bridge that spanned a canal where open-air restaurants spilled packed tables onto waterfront walkways. Small motorboats chugged along while gondolas glided serenely under the arch of the bridge. Zak wished he had the time to take it all in. He'd been told all his life what an amazing city Venice was – and now he was here he was too intent on getting safely to his destination to enjoy any of it.

He continued to use Foxhunt Rules: doubling back on himself, swerving down narrow alleys, crossing small hump-backed stone bridges over narrow canals, then turning and crossing straight back again, watching for anyone doing the same. Occasionally he'd slip into doorways, hide in the shadows and observe the people passing by. At other times, he'd pause outside shop fronts, pretending to be looking at the window displays while secretly eyeing the people behind him reflected in the glass.

The busy streets of Venice opened in front of him and closed behind him as he hurried on, giving him brief glimpses of ornate old churches and towering gothic buildings, colourful palazzos and crowded street markets.

Finally he ran out of a narrow alley and found a wide stretch of water in front of him. Low islands lined the horizon, weighed down by ancient buildings. The lagoon was alive with boats and waterbuses. He saw a white ticket office with a yellow sign that read FOND. NOVE.

Fondamente Nove.

The waterbus to Burano was about to leave. He searched the crowd for Switch. He wasn't there. Should he wait or should he go?

The last people boarded the waterbus. Still no sign of Switch.

Sorry, Switch, I can't wait. You're going to have to play catch-up.

Switch knew where Zak was heading. He'd follow for sure.

With one final display of caution, Zak waited until the vessel had already cast off and was moving away from the concrete jetty before sprinting forwards and jumping aboard.

Someone frowned at him and said, "*Sciocco ragazzo!*" as he walked past to find a seat.

He didn't know what it meant, but he guessed it probably wasn't complimentary.

He managed to squeeze in between two people and sit down. He twisted his head, looking back at the receding shoreline. Was anyone standing there looking cheesed off? He couldn't tell.

He took out the mobile phone, just to check he hadn't missed a call from Gabriel while he'd been running. He hadn't.

He turned around in his seat and looked out over the lagoon.

Soon, he wouldn't need the phone any longer.

Soon, he'd meet the elusive Agent Archangel, his brother's friend and ex-partner. The man who called himself Gabriel.

The sun was low in the sky by the time the waterbus chugged into its moorings on Burano. The boat trip across to the island of Torcello only took a few more minutes, but by then Zak's heart was pounding in anticipation of his upcoming encounter with Gabriel.

The island was flat and green, with ancient stucco buildings dotted about behind lush groves of trees. Despite the trickle of tourists, the place had a quiet, almost lonely, feel to it. In the distance, Zak saw what looked like a very old church with a red-tiled roof. Zak followed the signs and it wasn't long before he found himself walking uneasily through the palazzo ruins. The ruins seemed once to have been a monastery or a large church. The stone walls still reared up, but the windows showed only the sky, darkening now towards evening. Sad doorways led from nowhere to nowhere, and grass grew thick over the rubble of the fallen roofs.

He walked through the ruins for a while, starting at every person who came suddenly around a corner, or who he found standing admiring some broken chunk of statuary. An uneven set of red brick steps led to a network of linked under-chambers and corridors with low, curved ceilings and dusty, earth floors.

It was oddly cool down there, and it took Zak's eyes a little while to adjust to the twilight. He found himself walking the sunken hallways alone. It was also strangely silent under the ground; almost sinister.

"Hello, Zak." Despite the fact he'd been expecting to hear his voice for at least the last ten minutes, Zak was startled when Gabriel spoke. He stepped from a shadowed doorway where Zak could have sworn no one had been standing a moment ago.

His heart raced. Blood was pumping around his body as if it was turbo-charged. "Gabriel?" he gasped. It wasn't really a question. The tall, handsome young man standing in front of him had to be Gabriel. He had a deep tan and blond hair centre-parted and falling over dark eyes. He was wearing a T-shirt with a pale linen jacket and trousers. A camera hung around his neck and he had a backpack slung casually over one shoulder.

Basically, he looked like any one of a hundred thousand unremarkable tourists in their mid-twenties.

"You did well to get this far, Zak," said Gabriel. "You had plenty of opportunities to turn back. I'm impressed." His voice took on a sharp edge. "Were you followed?"

"I don't think so."

"Foxhunt Rules?"

Zak nodded.

Gabriel gave a quick, brief smile then turned, gesturing for Zak to follow him. They walked for a while until they came to a grassy place where the roof had fallen in and there was more light. Gabriel sat down on a chunk of rubble. "Padrone's goons are all over me," he said without any preamble. "I don't know what tipped them off." He looked up at Zak, standing in front of him. "They're not going to back off. Things could get messy, Zak. I just want to warn you in advance."

In advance? Was he kidding? Things had been messy since the Eiffel Tower incident. It was weird to finally be standing face-to-face with Agent Archangel. He hadn't really known what to expect. A few words of gratitude for trusting him, perhaps? Some understanding of how much Zak had put on the line to help him? But he got why there wasn't time for that kind of thing. He just wondered how much worse it was going to get now they were on Padrone's home turf.

"So, what do you want me to do?" Zak asked, pushing his thoughts aside. "Why am I here?"

"Because I need someone really fast to get to the top floor of the Banca Mondo building in San Marco," Gabriel explained. "That's where Padrone works – and that's where we're going to set a trap for Talpa."

Talpa was the mole's codename, Zak remembered.

"I've got a safe place where you can sleep tonight," Gabriel continued, "and tomorrow we'll spend the day scoping the building and working out exactly how you're to get in there. The mission is on for tomorrow night."

"I think not," said a voice from the shadows. A thickly accented Italian voice, dripping with menace. Gabriel leaped to his feet and Zak spun around. A man in a dark suit stepped from the cover of a wall. He was holding a gun.

"*Sparafucile!*" hissed Gabriel.

Zak's mind raced. Had he unwittingly brought the gunman here despite all his efforts?

The man walked slowly towards them, his arm outstretched, his gun at shoulder height. "Padrone sends his regards, Archangel," he said, smiling coldly. "Did you really think you could outwit him?" He glanced at Zak. "And who is this little *topo*? Is British Intelligence so desperate that they must recruit a *piccolo ragazzo* – a little boy – to do their dirty work for them?"

"Let him go, Sparafucile," said Gabriel. "He's not involved in this."

"Too late, Archangel," said Sparafucile. "I have already heard why he is here." He smiled coldly. "I have only one question – which of you would like to die first? And would anyone like to beg for mercy? I might enjoy that."

Zak glared at the man, his hands balling into fists – but Sparafucile was too far away to be taken down from where he was standing. Unless he came up with some ploy to give Gabriel time to act? A ploy that would probably get him a bullet in the head.

From the corner of his eye, Zak saw a sudden movement. Something whizzed through the air. It struck Sparafucile on the wrist. He yelled in pain as the gun spun out of his fingers.

The thing was a stone.

Zak reacted almost without thinking. He darted forwards, butting his shoulder hard under the man's ribcage. Sparafucile went down with a grunt.

Gabriel was on him in a moment, snatching at his collar with one hand and delivering a perfect karate chop to his neck. Sparafucile's body spasmed for a moment then became horribly still.

Zak stared down at him, breathing hard, feeling slightly sick.

A figure stepped from the shadows.

Switchblade.

He was holding another rock in his hand – presumably in case the first one hadn't done the trick.

Gabriel was on his feet again, crouched low, legs spread, watching Switch intently.

Switch dropped the stone and held his hands out. "I'm on your side," he said. "Project 17. Codename Switchblade. You can put away those lethal hands, Archangel, before someone else gets hurt."

Gabriel straightened up. He threw Zak a questioning look.

"He's telling the truth," Zak said. "We were together on the train. He followed me. There was a tracker on me."

"*What?*" Gabriel's eyes were furious. "You idiot! I told you to be careful!"

"Hey!" snapped Switchblade. "There's no harm done. The tracker is gone now. No one knows where we are."

He glanced at Sparafucile. "Except maybe some of Padrone's people." He looked sharply at Gabriel. "Who exactly is he, and who led him here, I wonder?"

"His name is Sparafucile,' said Gabriel. "He's one of Padrone's top hired guns." He frowned at Zak. "Sorry," he said. "I shouldn't have called you that. Padrone's people are everywhere right now. He may have been tailing me – I don't know."

Zak swallowed hard. "Is he dead?"

Gabriel nodded. "We'll have to hide the body. But if Padrone's people are this close, we're running out of time."

"Time to do what?" asked Switch. "Silver has put his life on the line for you. You've given him no proof about this mole, but he's trusted you all the way, and he's nearly been killed for it."

"We might all be killed before this thing is done," said Gabriel. "That's the price we must be willing to pay." He held Switchblade's gaze. "There's a mole high up in British Intelligence, and I mean to bring him down. Are you going to help me do that, or were you sent to stop me?"

Switch stared at him. "You think I'm working with a traitor?" he said coldly.

"Can you prove you're not?" Gabriel responded.

Zak didn't like the tension that was building between

Switch and Gabriel.

"Listen, you guys, this isn't helping," he broke in, stepping between them. He looked at Gabriel. "I'd trust Switch with my life, okay?" He turned to Switch. "We've come this far – let's just go with it."

There was a moment when Zak wasn't sure which way it would go, then both Switch and Gabriel nodded.

"We'd better get this character out of sight before someone strolls in on us," said Switch, gesturing towards Sparafucile's body.

"Agreed," said Gabriel. "And then I'll take you to a safe house where we can finalize our plans." He looked at Zak. "Padrone is too close," he said. "We can't afford to wait. The mission has to go ahead tonight."

They were in a small room high in an old building that overlooked one of Venice's many canals. Night had fallen, and the city was ablaze with coloured lights and noisy with tourists. Below the window, Zak could hear the slow, steady splash of a gondola gliding past. A voice sang a lilting melody. A cat yowled and anther voice called out roughly. But, up here, the lights were dimmed and all was quiet and subdued. It was unbearably tense.

Zak still felt shocked and sickened by the swift way in which Gabriel had killed the Italian gunman. It was as though he hadn't thought about it for even a second. *Wham!* Dead! Just like that. Zak found himself wondering whether his long-lost brother was capable of acting the same way. Did Jason have the ability to kill so easily, so . . . efficiently?

Gabriel sat at a small desk with a laptop open in front of him. Switch and Zak were behind him, looking at a schematic of the Banca Mondo building in the Campi Merceri, a square just north of the huge Basilica di San Marco. They had already been shown photographs on-screen. From the outside, the five-storey bank looked like one of a thousand old Venetian buildings, built from white stone and decorated all over with columns and arches and pillars. But it did have some unique features – there was a big ornate clock face over the main entrance, and on the flat roof was a huge sculpture that consisted of a large metal bell with a statue on either side of a man wielding a long-handled hammer in one raised arm. Apparently, on the hour every hour through the day, an old clockwork mechanism cranked into action and the men's arms would swing down to hammer out the time on the bell.

But the seventeenth-century façade hid the fact that

the whole building had recently been gutted and fitted with a new steel framework to house the offices of the international merchant bank, Banca Mondo.

Gabriel tapped a key and the 3D schematic of the newly renovated building turned slowly on the screen, its walls and floors, lift shafts and stairways showing as a complex mesh of interweaving lines.

"Before the Banca Mondo took over, you could have got into the place with a bent paperclip," Gabriel told them. "But now they've installed one of the most sophisticated security systems in the entire city. We need to get in there, but Padrone's people will be on highest alert now. To give us a better chance, I've put out some useful disinformation."

Zak frowned. *Disinformation?* Oh yes, he remembered now – disinformation meant lies intended to deceive an enemy.

"I've sent some coded messages that suggest we'll be targeting Padrone at his home," Gabriel continued. "They don't realize I know they broke the code. They believe the Banca Mondo building is virtually impregnable, so they should believe the messages are genuine. I've said we intend to kidnap Padrone tonight from his home and take him to London for a full debriefing."

"So, while his thugs are busy at Padrone's house, we

move in at the bank," said Switch. "Clever. Unless they're right and the building can't be broken into." He leaned over Gabriel's shoulder. "Can the system be compromised?" he asked. "Is there any way to shut it down or mess with it? I'm up to speed on the latest computer tech for breaking even the most sophisticated systems."

"I don't think so." Gabriel stood up, gesturing to the chair. "But be my guest, the specs are all there."

Switch sat down and began tapping at the keyboard. Zak watched as a whole bunch of complicated sub-screens began to pop up.

"Any luck?" Zak asked after Switch had been studying the monitor for a few minutes.

"Absolutely," Switch said flatly. "Give me two weeks and a few pointers from Bug and I could maybe just about break the system." He looked at Gabriel. "You're right – there's no time for monkeying with it."

"The moment the outer perimeter of the building is breached, it goes into automated lockdown," Gabriel explained. "Metal shutters come down over the doors, steel mesh grilles cover all the windows and certain areas of the stairways and floors are electrified. It means that no one can get in or out of the building until the reset key has been entered into the control box and a specific ten-digit code typed on the keypad."

He looked from Zak to Switch. "The important thing for us is that, until the code is entered, no one can get *in*." He gave a grim half-smile. "Only two men hold copies of the reset key," he continued. "The president of the bank, Bernardo Bachino, who is currently attending a conference in Switzerland, and Dante Rizzo, his trusted deputy." He raised an eyebrow. "Anyone care to guess Dante Rizzo's secret alias?"

"Padrone," breathed Zak.

"You got it," said Gabriel. "Rizzo lives fairly close by, but I've calculated that it will take him at least ten minutes to get to the bank and disable the security measures so that the police can get inside and grab whoever is in there." He smiled. "Ten minutes is plenty of time for what I've got planned."

"So, Silver breaks in," Switch said slowly, as if thinking the thing through as he spoke. "The security system kicks in, closing off all the doors and windows and electrifying the floors. And this stays active till Dante Rizzo turns it off about ten minutes later." He frowned. "At which point the police swoop in and grab Silver, who has presumably been standing on a desk in reception so he doesn't get toasted by the electric floors. Have I got it right so far?"

"Not entirely," said Gabriel. "Only the lower halls and stairways are electrified – not the upper levels, and not the offices. And we have one thing in our favour. The system takes sixty seconds to lock the building down completely – starting from the ground floor up. If Zak gets a move on, he'll be up in Padrone's office on the fifth floor before the system has fully engaged." He opened a drawer in the desk and drew out a metal rod, about thirty centimetres long. "This is an amalgam of steel and osmium," he said. "It's the hardest thing on this planet next to diamonds." He handed it to Zak. It felt strangely heavy. "When you get to the top floor, stand this in a window frame. It's strong enough to hold the grille up so you can get out. Once you've done the business in Padrone's office, you exit via the window, get onto the roof and jump to the rooftop of the nearest building."

"And how far is that?" asked Switchblade.

"About ten metres," said Gabriel. He looked eagerly at Zak. "You can do that, can't you?"

"Ten metres?" said Zak. He had performed some pretty long jumps in his time, but he didn't think he'd ever managed ten metres. It wasn't possible, surely? It was way too far. He smiled and gave a casual flick of his head. "No problem," he said. "Piece of cake."

He saw Switch looking at him anxiously.

"So," he said, keeping his eyes on Gabriel, "what am I supposed to do in Padrone's office?"

CHAPTER **TWELVE**

VENICE.
CAMPI MERCERI.
03.20

A few lights were still glowing in the closed shops and restaurants that lined the square, but the Campi Merceri was completely deserted and strangely quiet in the small hours of the Venetian night.

The distant noises of the city only made the silence here seem more intense.

Three figures, little more than shadows among the

shadows, glided soft-footed under an arched walkway.

Zak was wearing his backpack. Inside were three things. The steel and osmium rod, a computer disk, and a small but lethal incendiary device that he was to set off in Padrone's office as soon as he'd completed his mission.

Zak was trying hard not to over-think what he had to do. Too much thinking only threw up a whole heap of ways in which things could go wrong. He'd been told that in basic training. Make your plan. Act on the plan. Don't try to second-guess yourself.

Easy to say . . .

A high stone arch led to the main entrance of the Banca Mondo, and covered walkways ran along the face of the building on either side. Beyond the arch, Zak could see the open-plan ground floor of the bank, brightly lit behind glass and steel doors and tall picture windows.

Gabriel's hand rested on Zak's shoulder. Zak had been so focused on the bank that the pressure made him jump a little. Every nerve, every muscle, every sinew in his body felt as if it was hot-wired and raring to go.

"Remember," whispered Gabriel. "Sixty seconds, bottom to top. The moment you get into Padrone's office, jam a window open or you're sunk."

Zak nodded impatiently. He'd been told all this. He just wanted to get on with it now. He just wanted it to be over.

Each of them had a mobile phone, set so they could be in constant three-way contact.

Gabriel gestured for Switch to stay back. Zak saw the concern in his friend's eyes, but he did his best to ignore it. He gave Switch a quick thumbs-up before following Gabriel towards the bank.

Don't worry. It'll be fine.

They moved in under the walkway and ran to the glass wall. It was so bright in there! Floodlit almost, laid out like any big bank, with two long rows of counters shielded by glass panels. Barriers of scarlet rope divided the marble floor into customer waiting areas. There were automated machines and plush couches. It all looked very exclusive and luxurious. Zak guessed that it attracted wealthy clients.

Gabriel indicated that Zak was to stay put as he ran in a crouch across the face of the bank. He kneeled under the huge window. He was also wearing a backpack. He took some things out and got busy. A few moments later, a small pack of explosive was taped to the bottom of the window. Gabriel spun out some thin wires, backing off towards Zak.

Gabriel twiddled the wires between his fingers then attached them to a small handheld device.

"Fire in the hold!" he murmured.

There was a bright flash, a bang and the crunch of broken glass.

"Go!" Gabriel barked.

Zak darted forwards. The smoke from the explosion was still billowing as he ran. A neat hole had been punched through the thick reinforced glass. Cracks radiated out like a spider's web, but the rest of the pane was holding.

As Zak dived headfirst through the hole and went rolling across the marble floor of the bank, the alarm went off.

It was loud! Like, ear-splittingly loud. The loudest thing Zak had ever heard. He could hardly think for the noise.

Sixty seconds.

He sprang to his feet and raced across the floor. There was a row of lifts along the wall – but Gabriel had told him that the lifts would be the first things to go into lockdown. There were double doors to one side. Beyond the doors was a stairway.

He heard a rattling, clanking noise behind him. He glanced over his shoulder. A series of steel mesh gates were coming down over the entrance, blocking the doors and windows. Steel shutters crashed over the lifts.

He sprinted for the double doors. The shutter was already descending. He wouldn't make it. Yes! He *would*. He flung himself to the floor, skidding along, crashing into the doors and rolling through just as the hard steel edge of the shutter hit the marble floor with a clang.

Talk about Indiana Jones!

He leaped to his feet and bounded up the stairs, deafened by the screaming of the alarm, aware of the clang and crash of shutters going down all around him, entombing him in here.

Halfway up the stairs he realized his mobile phone had fallen out of his pocket. He slammed on the brakes, leaning over the banister. Yes, there it was, lying by the doors. Surely he had a few seconds to go and get it?

But the phone started to sizzle and jump. For a moment he couldn't figure it out – then as the phone burst into flames, he realized what had happened. The floor had become electrified.

He pelted up the stairs, clinging onto the banister as he hit the landing, swinging around and going up in great four- or five-step leaps. He passed the first floor. The shutter already covered the doors that led from the stairwell.

He redoubled his efforts, going up the next flights as if he was being reeled up on a wire. The second-floor shutters were locked down as well. The system was beating him.

Focus. Concentrate.

He flung himself up the next flight of stairs – and suddenly his body and brain were locked together and he was in the zone.

Third floor. Shutters down.

Fourth floor. Shutters hitting the floor as he passed.

He flew up the final flights and hit the landing just as the shutter was dropping. No time to think, only to act. He hurled himself headlong across the floor, arms stretched out like a diver, sliding along the smooth polished stone tiles.

His hands hit the doors, pushing them open. He could hear the clanking of the shutter. It was coming down fast – only a few centimetres above him now.

And then disaster struck. His backpack caught on the shutter and he was brought to a sudden stop, halfway through the door.

He acted on pure instinct, twisting onto his side under the vice-like grip of steel. There was a grinding noise as the shutter shuddered to a stop. The steel and osmium rod in his backpack had become lodged between the bottom of the shutter and the floor.

Twisting his body, he jackknifed up, knees to his chest, back curved, arms reaching forwards. With a final supreme effort, he dragged himself out from under the shutter. He yanked the backpack free and the steel shutter hammered down behind him like a guillotine.

Breathing hard from fear rather than exertion, Zak scrambled to his feet and raced along the corridor. The blood was ringing in his head louder than the alarm siren. The doors up here were still accessible. He was a fraction of a second ahead of the security system.

He needed the fourth door on the left. That's what Gabriel had told him.

He saw the nameplate on the door.

Vice Presidente Dante Rizzo.

Gotcha!

As he opened the door, Zak heard the shutters crashing down all along the corridor. He leaped in as the shutter to Dante Rizzo's office dropped. The stairwell and hallway had been lit, but now he was in deep darkness.

He fumbled for a light switch, and as the fluorescent tubes blinked into action, he hurled himself at the window behind the desk. He grabbed the catch and hauled the window open. Rummaging in his backpack, he pulled out the steel and osmium road and jammed it in place a split second before the metal grille came down.

The grille slammed into the top of the slender rod. For a horrible moment, Zak was convinced the rod would break under the pressure. But it held. Through the window he could see the empty square far below. But he had no mobile to let the others know he was okay.

The alarm was still blaring, but not so loudly now, not from up on the top floor. Zak turned and ran to the desk. He threw himself into the black leather armchair and jabbed a finger at the computer keyboard. A moment later, the screen lit up with a picturesque scene of Venice by moonlight.

Zak took the computer disk from his backpack and fed it into the slot at the side of the machine.

He drummed his feet on the carpet, staring at the screen, waiting for something to happen. According to Gabriel, he would only have to follow on-screen instructions to get the job done.

The computer acknowledged the disk and displayed a small window. There was a search box, just as Gabriel had told him. He typed in the words he'd been given: **case vacanza**.

He pressed ENTER.

The words meant 'holiday homes'. Gabriel had told him nothing else about the file, except that he should attach it to the email that the disk would compel the computer to send.

The word '**Continue**' appeared.

Zak clicked. An email server appeared and a blank email opened, already showing a recipient, the address: a series of letters, symbols and numbers that meant nothing to him.

He typed the message that Gabriel had made him learn by heart. IMPERATIVE WE MEET FACE-TO-FACE IN LONDON TOMORROW. YOU HAVE BEEN COMPROMISED. YOUR LIFE AND LIBERTY DEPEND ON MEETING ME SO WE CAN GET YOU OUT.

Zak hesitated, trying to remember the rest. Gabriel had texted the message to him on his mobile phone in case he forgot it. A great help that was, now the phone had been deep-fried on the ground floor.

Think! Come on. You know this.

Yes!

MEET ME BY THE STATUE OF PETER PAN IN KENSINGTON GARDENS AT 20.00 HOURS TOMORROW.

Zak clicked on the Attach icon and attached the Case Vacanza file. He pressed SEND. There was a electronic whooshing sound and the email was gone.

How easy was that?

Now all he needed to do was set the incendiary device so that Padrone wouldn't know that his computer had been used to send a bogus message to the mole. Then he could get out of here.

Just as long as he could jump ten metres.

Forcing that uneasy thought away, Zak reached into the backpack and drew out the small plastic box that held the firebomb. Just open the lid, flip the switch and be out of there before the digital countdown went from two minutes to zero. Then, boom, burn, bye-bye to Padrone's office, desk, computer and all.

Zak laid the device in front of the computer module and took off the lid. Getting up, he reached a finger in and flipped the switch, ready to zip through the window the moment it went live.

He frowned. The digital countdown should have lit up.

It hadn't.

He flipped the switch back and forth a couple of times.

Nothing.

He grabbed a desk lamp and put it on, leaning in close to the device.

Two wires had come loose from two terminals.

"*Oh, no!*" he muttered under his breath.

Not good.

It must have happened when he'd almost got trapped under the shutter.

Two yellow wires.

Two terminals.

And a small plastic tube attached, packed with enough thermite to take this whole room out in one violent super-heated explosion.

If you hadn't dropped your mobile, you could have asked Gabriel what to do.

Yes. Thanks for that. Really helpful.

Zak stared at the wires, trying to work out which one belonged where. But it was impossible to tell. All he did know – and he really wished he *didn't* – was that if he wired it up wrong, the whole thing could go up in his face.

Two choices.

He heard noises from below, coming in through the open window. The screeching of tyres. Police sirens. Car doors slamming. People shouting.

The polizia had arrived – and in force by the sound of it.

There was no time left.

He reached in and pushed one of the wires back into one of the terminals. Not even thinking. Just taking a chance.

His body felt hot and chilly at the same time. It was an odd, unpleasant sensation. His hands trembled and he found he was taking short, shallow breaths. His skin felt prickly under his clothes.

He took the other wire between finger and thumb and slipped it back into the second terminal.

He gave a gasp of relief as the digital display lit up.

His eyes widened in alarm.

The display showed 00:08.

Eight seconds. Not two minutes – *eight seconds!*

00:07.

00:06.

"Silver? Come on, Silver." Switch's voice cracked with anxiety as he spoke into the mobile. "*Silver! Talk to me!*"

He looked at Gabriel. But Gabriel just shook his head and carried on staring across at the Banca Mondo building. The two of them were in cover on the far side of the square. The blare of the alarm filled the night. The shutters were coming down fast over the windows, floor by floor.

Switchblade was sure something had gone wrong. Why wasn't Quicksilver responding? Why couldn't they hear anything over the phone? He glared at Gabriel.

Had he sent Quicksilver to his death in that building? Had the electrified floors got him?

This whole crazy enterprise had been a mistake from the start. He should never have gone along with it. He should have put Quicksilver in a headlock and dragged him back to Fortress, no questions asked.

Gabriel's arm shot out, a finger jabbing upwards across the square. "Look!" Switch followed the line of the pointing finger. Up on the top floor, a window had opened. A pale hand placed a grey metal rod in the frame. A face showed for an instant and then was gone.

"He did it," gasped Gabriel, leaning against the wall as though his legs had gone to jelly underneath him. "He actually managed to get up there. Thank God – he had me really worried for while."

"It's not over yet," murmured Switch, eyeing the gap between the Banca Mondo and the nearest building. Ten metres to the closest rooftop. It was too far – maybe too far even for Quicksilver.

Seconds ticked by.

Switch heard police sirens, faint at first against the racket being kicked up by the bank's alarm, but rapidly getting closer and louder. Then there came the growl of motors and the screaming of tyres. Three police cars roared into the square. Two more joined them from the other side, slewing to a halt on the paving stones, their doors bursting open. Armed police officers ran towards the Banca Mondo, calling out, racing to block all possible exits.

An unmarked black car skidded to a halt in front of the bank. A heavy-set middle-aged man wearing a coat over pyjamas ran to the side of the building, flanked by police officers.

Padrone, for sure. That had been quick. Too quick.

The police officers lifted a metal hatch in the ground and the man knelt down and reached into the hole.

A few moments later, the bank's sirens cut out and the metal grilles over the doors and ground-floor windows began to clank upwards.

Switch glanced up just as an explosion sent a tongue of red flame spouting from the half-open window on the fifth floor. The sound of the detonation reverberated across the square.

The bomb had gone off.

But had Quicksilver got out in time?

CHAPTER **THIRTEEN**

Zak was beyond the zone. He was in a place where his body was working faster than his brain. The zone times ten. The *uber-zone*.

His mind hardly had time to register that something had gone catastrophically wrong with the timing mechanism before his body took him out of the window. He slipped under the metal grille, twisting in mid-air, snatching at the window frame with both hands as he turned. His feet came down on the outer sill. Knees bent, leg muscles contracted, bearing down hard on the stone sill, he released all the power in his legs, catapulting himself upwards.

His fingers grasped the lip of stone above him. His momentum took him up and over the edge. He sprawled face down on the flat roof.

The whole world seemed to shudder as the bomb went off in Padrone's office. Zak turned onto his back, seeing a spurt of red flame licking out into the night, watching the dark smoke roll and boil.

A few seconds slower and he would have been toast.

He got to his feet, wiping sweat out of his eyes. The huge metal bell with its two hammer-wielding statues towered over him, taking up the whole of the centre of the roof.

As the echoes of the explosion died away, he realized that the alarm had stopped. He knew what that meant. Padrone had disabled the security system. The police could get into the building now.

He gathered himself and jogged to the side of the roof. The moment had come. He stared across the crazy gap to the closest rooftop.

Ten metres.

Are you *kidding* me?

He looked over his shoulder. He guessed he had at most a twelve-metre run-up to the jump.

He ran to the far edge of the roof.

Focus. Concentrate. Get in the zone.

He hesitated, his heart going way too fast, the blood howling in his head.

It was now or never.

He gathered himself and ran. The statues of the two men loomed over him, at least five metres tall, watching him with their blind metal eyes.

Faster. Arms pumping. Legs rising and falling like pistons. Eyes on the far roof. In the zone.

At the last possible moment he knew he wouldn't make it.

It wasn't cowardice that stopped him – it was the absolute clear-headed certainty that he'd fall short; that he'd plunge to his death.

He skidded to a halt on the rim of the long drop, gasping for breath, his head pounding.

He couldn't do it. The police would find their way up to the roof and he'd be caught.

No!

Something in him simply wouldn't accept that it was hopeless. He stared at the great bell with its two huge statues.

A ridiculous idea popped into his head.

He jumped up onto the metal plinth that supported the statues. He stood under one of the great iron men.

The statue's knees were at the same height as his head. The giant man was holding up the hammer in one hand, its arm jointed at the shoulder. He assumed there must be some kind of mechanism inside the statue that worked to swing the arm and strike the bell on the hour. Zak guessed the hammer must be at least two metres long. He began to climb.

He boosted himself up onto the statue's shoulder. It hadn't been a difficult climb and he wasn't even out of breath. Setting his back against the cold metal head, he braced himself and kicked at the arm.

There was a dull clunk. Gripping hard onto the statue's shoulder with both hands he kicked again, harder this time, really going for it.

Clang.

No movement.

Again he kicked, both feet striking the statue's upper arm, the impact jarring Zak's whole body.

Again. Sweat trickled down his face and back. Pain grew in his feet and legs, his fingers going numb where he was gripping the metal ridges of the huge shoulder.

And then he felt it. The surge of power that he'd only felt once before. His head throbbed, the world swam in front of his eyes. A weird, unnerving strength flooded through him.

He could feel the arm moving now. Jerking away under his feet.

Kick! Kick! *Kick!*

And suddenly his feet hit empty air. He almost fell, but he just managed to stop himself. He heard a low, dull clang from beneath him. He stared down. The arm had come loose. It had dropped to the roof.

He caught his breath and slithered down the statue, his legs trembling, his head spinning. He dragged the arm to the edge of the roof, feeding off strange, uncanny reserves of energy. He heaved the arm around so that the hand rested on the lip of the roof and the hammer jutted out into the air.

Two metres of solid metal, hanging over the long drop.

Zak ran to the far side of the roof. He turned and, without hesitating for even a fraction of a second, shot forwards. His eyes were on the hammer's head, a grey stepping stone in the dark night. He hit the arm at top speed, bounding along it, striking up off the clenched fist.

One foot came down halfway along the handle of the hammer, giving him extra lift and momentum. His other foot met the head of the hammer and he sprang forwards. The wind rushed in his ears. The stars wheeled over his head. The pale edge of the far roof came rushing towards him.

He landed hard, his legs scissoring as he stumbled across the roof. He heard laughter ringing in his ears. Relieved laughter that was coming from his own mouth.

He dropped to his knees, still laughing breathlessly, and then crashed onto his face. Time passed in a dark haze. He hurt all over. Then he was vaguely aware of being turned over. A pale face stared down at him. A muffled voice boomed in his ears. He was lifted up and carried into darkness.

"It was a good thing the police weren't watching the roof, Silver," said Switchblade. "If they'd seen what was going on up there, we'd never have got to you first."

Zak was slumped in an armchair in that same dimly lit room overlooking the canal. He wasn't entirely sure how he'd got there. He must have passed out at some point. Outside the window, the sky was the pale greyish blue of dawn.

"How are you feeling now?" Zak turned his woozy head at the sound of Gabriel's voice.

"Fine," he murmured.

"Really?"

"No . . ." The truth was that he felt burned out, drained and frazzled, but he didn't have the strength to say so.

"Did you send the email, Zak?" Gabriel said urgently.

Zak's mind was so fuzzy that he had to think hard for a moment to work out what Gabriel was talking about.

"Yes," he said slowly. "Yes, I did."

Gabriel's hand came down on his shoulder. "Excellent."

Zak groaned.

"Sorry – I guess you ache a bit."

A bit?

He felt as though he'd been put through a fast spin cycle in a washing machine then thrown under a steamroller.

"Listen, take it easy for a while," said Gabriel. "Switch will look after you. I'm going out to make some arrangements to get the two of you out of here. You did well. You did really well."

Zak lifted a leaden arm to acknowledge the compliment, one thumb up.

He heard the door close.

"Silver?" Switch's voice was full of concern. "Do you want anything?"

"Yes," Zak said softly. "I want to go home."

MARCO POLO AIRPORT, VENICE.
LOCAL TIME: 07:15

Zak, Switchblade and Gabriel were in the departure lounge of the airport, waiting for the announcement that the flight they had booked that morning for the two Project 17 agents was ready to board. Both Zak and Gabriel were wearing hoodies with the hoods up to shade their faces.

Gabriel's eyes were constantly darting to and fro, but so far they hadn't encountered any trouble.

"It's going to take a while for you to get to London," Gabriel told them. "I've booked you flights via Bucharest, Prague and Amsterdam. Padrone's men know Zak's face. If they manage to follow him, I don't want him leading them straight to London – not until we know we've hooked the mole."

"And what are you going to do?" asked Zak. He still felt wrung out, but the exhaustion of earlier that morning had worn off a little. Sleep would be good though. A nice little sleep. For maybe five or six days.

"My cover here is blown for sure," said Gabriel. "I've called in a few favours. I'll be taking a plane to Cairo

– I'll lie low there with some friends for a while. Then I'll await instructions from MI5."

"You're not coming back to London?" asked Zak.

Gabriel shook his head. "Not unless I'm summoned by my boss," he said. "My training is in deep cover. I work best in the field."

"How do we contact you?" asked Switchblade. "We'll want to give you a heads-up if the mole is found."

"Don't worry," said Gabriel. "If we get him, I'll hear about it."

"And if we don't?" Zak asked.

Gabriel's eyes flashed. "Then we start again," he said. He gave a quick smile. "Don't sweat it, Zak – the plan will work and Talpa will be finished."

Switch pointed to the departures screen. "We're boarding," he said. He shook Gabriel's hand. "Come on, Silver. Let's get moving."

Zak hesitated, looking into Gabriel's face, his head full of questions he had no time to ask. Gabriel knew his brother. He'd worked with him. Trained him.

What's Jason like? Is he a football fan? What kind of music does he listen to? Does he like free running? Does he have time for those kinds of things at all?

Is there any way to get in touch with him?

Does he even remember he had a baby brother?

It was too late.

"Go," said Gabriel, nodding to Zak. "You'll miss your plane."

Reluctantly, Zak turned and followed Switch.

The chances were that Agent Archangel wouldn't have let on even if he'd known the answers to Zak's questions. All the same, as Zak walked with Switch towards the gate, he looked back at Gabriel with an ache inside him that hurt like a punch in the gut.

THE HOME OFFICE, WESTMINSTER, LONDON.

Colonel Hunter stood in front of a large oak desk in a wood-panelled room with carpet-to-ceiling bookshelves. His back was straight and his face unreadable.

John Mallin sat behind the desk, his hands tweaking a sheaf of documents in an open folder. At his side stood Lieutenant Colonel McDermott. There was no expression on McDermott's face, but Colonel Hunter thought he saw a gleam of triumph in the heavy-lidded eyes.

John Mallin spoke. "In the light of your inability to discover the location of Agents . . . " He consulted the papers in front of him '. . . of Agents Quicksilver and

Switchblade, the Home Secretary, in consultation with the Prime Minister, has decided to suspend you as Control of Project 17." The eyes flickered over Colonel Hunter's impassive face. "The suspension begins immediately, Colonel Hunter. Lieutenant Colonel McDermott will be temporarily taking over command of Project 17, subject to a full review of the facts."

John Mallin closed the folder. "You will be given the opportunity to defend your actions in the full committee hearing that will take place in due course." He leaned back in his chair. "Do you have anything to say, Colonel?"

"No," said Colonel Hunter, his voice clipped but quite calm. "You've made the situation perfectly clear." Without even a glance at McDermott, he turned on his heel and marched from the room.

As he stalked down the corridor, he let a small fraction of his anger out by punching the wall. Hard.

Nursing bruised knuckles, he pushed through the main door and stormed down the steps towards the official car park on the other side of the street.

He climbed into his car and started the engine.

He paused, his hands on the wheel, staring through the windscreen.

What now?

A movement reflected in his rear-view mirror caught his eye. He twisted around as two heads popped up from the back seat.

"What the . . . ?"

"Sorry to startle you, Control," said Switch. "We didn't want anyone else to see us."

The Colonel's eyes remained unreadable as he looked from Switchblade to Quicksilver and then back again.

"This had better be good," he growled.

"Oh, it is," said Zak with a grin. "It really is!"

CHAPTER **FOURTEEN**

KENSINGTON GARDENS, LONDON.
20.00

Zak and Switchblade and Colonel Hunter stood silent
and still behind a dense barrier of leaves and branches.
They had been hiding in the thick hedgerow for thirty
minutes already, waiting in the growing twilight. Not
speaking. Hardly moving. Tense and hyper-alert for any
movement.

Peering through the hedge, Zak could make out the
circle of clipped grass with the tall bronze statue in

the middle. Peter Pan, standing on a plinth shaped like a tree trunk covered all over with small animals and dancing fairies.

A few people had come and gone over the past thirty minutes. A couple of children had climbed the bronze trunk to have their photos taken. But as the evening descended, the ring of grass had become deserted.

Switch nudged Zak and showed him his Mob. The screen was showing 20:04. If Talpa had received the email that Zak had sent, he should already be here.

But what if the mole didn't show? Colonel Hunter had been prepared to believe their story, but if Talpa didn't make an appearance, what then? What if somehow Padrone had worked out what had happened and warned the mole to keep away? Zak preferred not to dwell on that too much. That would mean deep, deep trouble, he guessed. For everyone.

Zak tried to stretch his aching limbs. The leaves shook and Colonel Hunter shot him a forbidding look.

"Sorry," Zak mouthed, becoming still again. He'd just have to live with the cramp. Switch was staring through the leaves, his forehead puckered. Zak guessed Switch was thinking the same as him.

Will Talpa come?

Time passed. The evening drew in.

Zak sneaked a look at Switch's Mob.

20:15.

It wasn't going to happen. The mole would never come.

A muscle was jumping on Colonel Hunter's jaw.

"Time?" the Colonel whispered, his eyes fixed on the statue.

"Twenty-eighteen," murmured Switch.

Colonel Hunter breathed heavily.

"A few more minutes?" Zak begged. It couldn't be over. Not yet. Not like this.

Someone pushed through the trees on the far side of the clearing and moved into the circle of grass. Hidden from sight by the bronze stump, they walked onto the ring of stones that surrounded the statue. Shoes clicked, then were silent. Whoever it was, they were standing on the other side of the statue, behind the bronze tree trunk. Two more minutes ticked past. The unseen figure didn't move.

Talpa. It had to be Talpa.

Colonel Hunter gave Zak and Switchblade the nod. The three of them broke cover and walked towards the statue.

"Stay right where you are," called the Colonel.

Zak heard a soft gasp. Shoes clicked rapidly on the stones as the figure darted to one side. Colonel Hunter sprang after the fleeing shape, his sudden burst of speed taking Zak entirely by surprise. Hunter might be an old guy, but he could certainly move when he needed to.

Colonel Hunter caught the fugitive by the coat sleeve. The figure spun around, the face angry and scared. Zak's eyes widened in amazement.

It was Margaret Pearce.

"Colonel Pearce!" Zak gasped, hardly able to believe what he was seeing.

"Unbelievable!" murmured Switchblade as Margaret Pearce struggled to get free of Colonel Hunter's vice-like grip.

"What are you doing, Peter?" she demanded. "Let go of me this instant."

"Cut it out," snapped the Colonel. "It's over, Talpa."

"What is this?" said Colonel Pearce. "You're talking nonsense."

"Give it up, Margaret," Colonel Hunter said firmly. "We know everything."

"I sent the email message from Padrone telling you to come here," said Zak, looking into Colonel Pearce's eyes. "It was a trap, and you walked straight into it!"

Colonel Pearce's eyes blazed with fury.

"Damn you!" she snarled, her lips twisting. "You little street rat!"

"Charming," murmured Switchblade.

Zak raised an eyebrow. "That's *Agent* Street Rat to you!" he said coolly. "And you're busted, you traitor!"

Zak stood in front of Colonel Hunter's desk, white-faced and wincing a little as the Colonel read out a long list of disciplinary breaches he'd stacked up during his unauthorized mission to Venice.

" . . . and any agent going away without the leave of his commanding officer will be dismissed from the Service immediately, and without leave to appeal," concluded the Colonel, closing the file.

He looked up at Zak. His face was stern, but there was no anger in his eyes.

Zak swayed on his feet. His legs felt watery and his stomach churned.

His life was about to be blown apart. Despite everything he'd done, despite helping to reveal the mole, he was going to be thrown out of Project 17. The injustice of it burned in his stomach, making him feel physically sick.

Just say it, Control. Just say the words and get it over with.

Colonel Hunter leaned back in his chair, his eyes fixed on Zak's face.

"I'm quite sure that if other people were running Project 17, that would be exactly the course they'd take," said the Colonel quietly. "But other people are *not* running this department, much as they'd like to. I am."

Zak wasn't quite sure he had understood. He blinked at the Colonel.

"You're not kicking me out?" he asked tentatively.

"I am not," said the Colonel.

Relief flooded through Zak's body. He was off the hook! His life wasn't about to be ruined after all.

"But I am going to formally reprimand you for dragging Bug into your little escapade," Colonel Hunter continued, his eyebrows lowered. "I've already done the same to Switchblade. You will both have demerit marks on your permanent records." His forefinger tapped his desk. "Project 17's protocols and chain of command are here for a reason, Quicksilver," he continued, but his voice was gentler now. "I've read your mission report. There are several occasions when you could have been killed."

"But I wasn't, was I?" Zak added hopefully.

The Colonel's steely expression silenced him. "Agent Quicksilver, if you do anything like this again, I will throw you out of my department so quickly even *your* feet won't touch the ground," he growled. "Am I making myself perfectly clear?"

"Yes, sir," mumbled Zak. "Sorry, sir."

"Dismissed."

Zak hesitated. "But . . ."

"But *what*?" asked Colonel Hunter. "How is it that you never leave my office without saying '*but*'?"

Zak couldn't be sure, but was there the faintest trace of a smile at the corner of the Colonel's mouth?

"Gabriel . . . I mean, Archangel, he never told me what was in that Case Vacanza file he asked me to attach to the email."

"It was the full list of all of Padrone's operatives working in Europe and America," said the Colonel. "It was attached as an undeletable file, so Colonel Pearce was unable to wipe it from her computer."

"That's good, isn't it?" said Zak.

"That's very good," agreed the Colonel. "Teams have been sent out and many of Padrone's people have already been scooped up. The rest are compromised and will need to go into hiding. This has put Padrone's operations back by several years."

"Outstanding!" said Zak with a smile. His efforts had cracked Padrone's gang wide open. Way to go!

"This is a major achievement," said Colonel Hunter.

"But Padrone wasn't working alone. He was the Italian operative of a terrorist organization with a global reach – an organization that still threatens us all."

"Is Reaperman involved?" Zak asked, remembering the name of the terrorist mastermind who had given the order to kill his parents.

"He is," said the Colonel. "But I'm not at liberty to tell you more than that. Some information is secret way above your rank, Quicksilver."

"Is Jason involved in working against him?" Zak blurted.

Colonel Hunter gazed at him for a few moments. "We're *all* working to bring Reaperman's organization down," he said. "You should go now, Quicksilver. You look like you need some sleep."

Zak turned and headed for the door.

"Zak," called the Colonel. Zak spun around, startled by the use of his real name. Colonel Hunter never used his real name.

The Colonel was leaning forwards behind his desk, looking shrewdly at him, his face solemn. "Don't go looking for your brother," he said. "When the time is right, the two of you will meet, you have my promise on that." He lowered his eyes, took a folder from his in-tray and opened it. "Dismissed," he said.

This time Zak knew better than to say 'but'.

Switch was waiting for him in the corridor.

"How'd it go?" Switch asked as they walked along together.

"Not too bad," said Zak. "But if I ever do anything like that again, I'm done for."

Switch grinned at him. "Me too." He paused, looking hard at Zak. "I just want to get one thing clear," he said. "Next time you decide to go rogue, tell me in advance so I don't have to chase halfway across Europe to catch up with you."

"Catch up with me?" laughed Zak. "You couldn't catch up with me if you chased me on a turbo-charged rocket."

"Is that so?" Switch made a playful grab for him, but Zak dodged aside and went haring down the corridor, yelling with laughter.

"I'll get you!" shouted Switch, racing after him.

"In your dreams!" Zak called back, a smile spreading across his face. "In your tiny little dreams!"

Turn the page for a sneak preview of Zak Archer's next mission:

Adrenaline Rush

CHAPTER **ONE**

HOLLYWOOD, CALIFORNIA.
FORTY-FIFTH DAY OF SHOOTING THE
MOVIE *ADRENALINE RUSH*.
LOCATION OF SHOOT: BENEDICT CANYON.

"Action!"

Zak was jogging on the spot, loosening his limbs, getting his body ready. At the sound of the director's voice, he snapped into focus and raced forwards. He ignored the camera operators and the swinging boom mikes and all the other people out of shot. He concentrated on the point where a narrow side street opened out to the long slope of the main road.

The bus would appear any moment now.

He could hear it coming – engine gunning, wheels on tarmac.

He was almost at his mark – the chalk line on the road that meant he was in view of the cameras.

The yellow school bus came barrelling down the hill, passing the end of the side street in a flash. Zak grinned, loving this. He leaned into his run, putting on a spurt of speed that took him into shot.

The bus was packed with seven-year-old kids. Zak could hear them yelling their heads off just like the director had told them to. "You're really scared, okay? The bus driver has had a heart attack. The bus is running out of control. Plenty of yelling and screaming, guys."

Zak hared out onto the main road, swerving to follow the careering bus. He saw panicky faces at the windows, fists beating on the glass, mouths stretched wide. The kids were really getting into it.

He'd been told to make it look good. Not too easy. To make it seem as if the bus was getting away from him. Don't worry about facial expressions – if we get a good shot of your face, we'll strip it out for the real actor in post-production.

Zak was just the stand-in, the stunt person. Because Zak could do the running for real. And that was what this action movie was all about – reality!

He slowed a little, letting the bus gain a lead on him. The director wanted effort and drama, and Zak was prepared to give it to him. After all, it wasn't every day he got asked to appear in a Hollywood blockbuster.

The voice of Grayson Clarke, the director, sang out in his earpiece. "That's great, Zak – now go for it."

"On it!" Zak moved up a gear, chasing the bus for real now, seeing the kids' faces staring out of the back window as he drew closer. Then he caught up and ran alongside the bus, spotting the cameras following the action out of the corner of his eye.

The door opposite the driver's seat was open. He gave a final burst of speed.

This was the tricky bit. He had to reach for the rail and pull himself on board. He'd been practising for the last two days with some of the professional stunt men. If he got it wrong and fell on his face, not only would he feel like a total idiot, but they'd have to start the scene from scratch. The producer, Elton Dean, wouldn't be happy. He was constantly marching around the set telling everyone that time was money.

Concentrate! Zak told himself. *Get it right.*

Zak snatched hold of the rail and boosted himself up onto the lowest step of the bus.

Perfect.

"That's excellent, Zak!" Grayson Clarke's voice was in his ear again. "Keep up the energy level. You're doing fine work."

"No problem," Zak said, speaking into the tiny mike that was attached to the lapel of his leather jacket.

The stunt driver – a really nice guy called Chet – was slumped over the wheel of the bus just as he'd been instructed.

Heart attack. Foot jammed down on the gas pedal. Bus out of control. Arrgh! Who will save the day?

Zak flung himself onto the steps, his ears now filled with the screaming of the kids. He had to admire their energy. Somewhere among them was Elton Dean's own nephew, Brandon Fine. Zak had met him briefly – a mouthy little kid with plenty of attitude.

Zak found his balance on the speeding bus then approached the driver. *Shake him by the shoulders. Yell in his ear.* "Are you okay, mister?" His voice wasn't being recorded, so it didn't really matter, but the director said it would help him 'keep in the moment' if he followed the script.

Chet was a real pro. He showed no signs of life as Zak grabbed him and hauled him out of the seat. There was blood on the front of Chet's shirt. That was weird. Zak hadn't been told there'd be blood.

"Keep the action moving, Zak," came Grayson Clarke's voice in his ear.

"I'm on it. " Zak assumed they'd explain about the blood later. He dragged Chet from the seat and let him slump on the floor between the driver's station and the steps. Then Zak jumped into the seat, grabbed the big steering wheel in both hands and stamped down hard on the brakes.

Oh, yes! This was the movies!

The bus didn't slow. Zak stared between his knees. The brake was marked with a big X so he couldn't get it wrong. He stamped again on the pedal marked X.

The bus just kept on going. In fact, it was speeding up now as the hill became steeper.

"Zak, you can stop the bus now," Grayson Clarke instructed.

"I'm trying to," Zak replied. He put his foot down again on the brake. It felt strangely loose, as if it wasn't connected to anything.

"Zak, you've passed your mark – stop the bus!" the director shouted.

"It's not working!" This wasn't in the script. What was he supposed to do?

Zak could hear Grayson Clarke. He was speaking to someone else now, but not bothering to cover the mike. "Amateurs!" he growled. "We should never have used amateurs." Zak started to feel worried. The director thought this was *his* fault.

Zak nudged Chet with his foot. "Chet, something's gone wrong," he shouted above the racket the kids were kicking up. "The brake isn't working! Chet! I can't stop the bus. *Chet!*"

He gave the stuntman a hard kick. The slumped body rolled onto its side on the floor of the bus. Zak saw that the patch of blood on Chet's shirtfront was larger now. And there was more blood on the floor.

He was beginning to get a bad feeling about this. But then, this was the movies – you couldn't believe anything you saw in the movies. It was all special effects . . . wasn't it?

"Hey, you chump, stop the bus!" Zak glanced over his shoulder at the sound of the angry voice. It was Brandon Fine. He was standing up and glaring at Zak from the middle of the bus. Zak didn't much like Brandon – he was seven going on thirty-five and ever since he'd turned up on location he'd been talking as if he was running the entire shoot. That's what comes of being the nephew of a Hollywood movie producer, Zak guessed.

"How dumb *are* you?" Brandon demanded. "You missed the mark, genius!" The other kids had stopped acting as well. They were staring at him, confused now.

"Calm down," Zak called to them. "Everything's fine."

"What a loser!" Brandon said, rolling his eyes.

Zak had more important things to do than argue with a stroppy seven year old.

Keeping one hand on the steering wheel, he leaned over and felt for the carotid artery on Chet's neck.

Nothing. No pulse. Chet was dead.

Zak's heart punched against his ribs. This was real.

He didn't want to panic the kids. They mustn't know what had happened. The footbrake had failed, but he wasn't out of options yet. He snatched hold of the handbrake and yanked at it. It moved easily in his hand, connected to nothing. Useless. What was going on here?

He had one last idea. He twisted the keys in the ignition and pulled them out.

The engine kept going, the bus hurtled onwards. He could hear Grayson Clarke's voice yelling in his ear, "Get Chet to stop the bus!"

He ignored the director. He couldn't think of anything to say that wouldn't freak the kids out.

Grayson Clarke was still yelling. "What are you waiting for?"

Will you shut up; I'm trying to think.

Zak gripped the steering wheel, his knuckles white. He was on his own with this – he had to come up with a way of stopping the bus. It wasn't easy with the road whipping away under the wheels and the hill getting steeper by the second. Some of the kids had started whimpering.

"Everything's fine!" Zak shouted back to them. "Just stay in your seats and hold tight."

He dropped his chin, trying to get his mouth as close to the mike as possible.

"The brakes aren't working," he said, hoping the kids wouldn't be able to hear him. "Chet can't help." Zak's voice died in his throat. He had just spotted something that set his heart pounding.

There was a small neat hole high in the windscreen, close to the driver's rear-view mirror. A hole no bigger than his little finger, with a spiderweb of cracks around it.

A bullet hole.

Chet had been shot dead and the bus had been sabotaged. For some reason someone wanted to put these kids in real danger. Zak clamped his fingers around the wheel, staring ahead, trying to come up with a plan.

The long hill descended for about another 500 metres before it levelled out and met the main four-lane highway. Zak could see the cars and trucks streaming past in both directions. If he couldn't stop the bus, it would smash right into the traffic.

Zak didn't have time to be stunned or scared or freaked out. He had to do something. And quickly.

The long hill began to curve a little and Zak saw there was a solid stone wall running down one side. The shred of a plan came into his mind. Grayson Clarke was still shouting in his ear, but he couldn't let himself be distracted. He ripped out the earpiece. Behind him, some of the kids were crying and sobbing – they'd figured out that something had gone wrong. Even Brandon had gone quiet.

Ignore them. Concentrate.

Zak turned the steering wheel, driving the bus towards the edge of the road. He gritted his teeth, hoping he wasn't about to get them all killed. The wall loomed closer. He eased the wheel around a fraction more.

The bus shuddered and shook as the front bumper made contact with the wall. The wheel juddered in Zak's hands. There was a screaming noise as metal grazed against stone.

Carefully. Not too hard. Gritting his teeth, Zak kept

the wheel locked, holding the bus against the wall. The grinding and screeching noise filled the bus.

"Get on the floor! Cover your faces!" Zak yelled. Kids flung themselves out of their seats, falling in heaps into the aisle and between the seats.

The sound of metal on stone was mind-shredding. Zak's whole body shook. He saw sparks and shards of stone flying into the air. The side of the bus was being ripped apart.

But it seemed to be working. The friction was beginning to slow the bus down.

The jolting in his arms was almost too painful to bear, but he refused to give in. Using every ounce of strength, he leaned against the wheel. Pieces of stone smashed through the windows, ricocheting all around. Showers of sparks spewed upwards. There was a horrible burning smell – hot metal and smouldering rubber.

Still Zak struggled with the wheel. The highway was only a hundred metres away now, filled with racing traffic.

A block of stonework jutted out from the wall. Zak just had time to see that it was one side of a gateway before the bus struck it. The windscreen disintegrated and chunks of stone cascaded into the bus. He ducked, feeling them hitting him and bouncing off. The impact caused the nearside of the bus to buckle, punching sharp-edged pieces of metal perilously close to Zak's legs.

The bus slewed around and tipped dangerously. For a moment Zak was afraid the whole thing would topple onto its side. Then it righted itself, crashed down on its wheels and came to a screeching halt.

Gasping with relief, Zak collapsed over the steering wheel.

He felt as though every bone in his body had been jarred loose. He felt like throwing up. His body ached.

But he had done it.

The sound of kids screaming roused him. He sat up and looked over his shoulder. Flames were licking around the outside of the bus. The friction must have set something on fire.

He staggered to his feet. "Come on," he yelled over the screaming. "We have to get out of here." Zak reached down and pulled Chet's limp body to one side. The kids began to tumble forwards, barging and jostling as they fought to get through the doors. They looked utterly terrified as Zak guided them off the bus.

The flames were rising now, advancing through the broken windows. The bus was filling with smoke. Zak coughed, blinking, his eyes stinging. He caught the last kid by the shoulder. A blonde girl with a ponytail and huge frightened blue eyes.

"Is there anyone else back there?" he asked her.

She stared at him for a moment then ripped herself free and dived down the steps.

Zak peered into the billowing smoke.

"Anyone there?" he shouted. He could hardly see, and his ears were still ringing from the noise of the crash. "*Anyone?*"

He crouched, trying to get down where the smoke was less thick. He could see a few bags and coats strewn across the floor. He saw a bundle about halfway down. Jammed between the seats. A coat?

"Hey!"

Was that a voice he could hear back there? The crackling of the flames made it hard to be sure.

He had done a firefighting course in training. He tried to remember what he'd been taught. Keep low in a smoke-filled room was one lesson he remembered very well. He flattened himself on his belly and edged forwards.

Coughing, and with streaming eyes, Zak headed for the bundle. The flames were leaping yellow and red through the pall of smoke. He could feel the heat on his face, scorching his clothes. Grimacing, he moved closer and reached under the seat.

There was a hand. He opened his mouth to say something reassuring, but found he couldn't speak. His breath was coming in choking gasps and he was almost blinded. He closed his fingers around the wrist and pulled, dragging the child along with him.

He was close to the exit now. The metal ridge of the top step was under his feet. He got to his knees, retching and unable to see much more than a dark blur. He could hear the boy coughing. He must have been knocked unconscious – but he was coming around.

Zak grabbed the limp bundle under the arms and stumbled down the steps, falling, turning so the kid didn't hit the tarmac first.

He could hear people yelling. Feet running. Someone took the kid from his arms. Someone else picked Zak up and carried him away from the bus.

"I'm okay," he panted. "Let me down."

He was put onto his feet.

"Chet is still in there," someone else shouted. "We have to get him out."

Zak swayed, his lungs hurting, his vision blurred. He rubbed the smoky tears out of his eyes.

"He's dead," he gasped.

"Are you sure?"

"He was shot," said Zak.

"He was *what*?"

Zak's head was swimming. "Someone shot him through the windscreen," he gasped. "And someone wrecked the brakes." He wiped his grimy sleeve across his face. "This wasn't an accident – this was deliberate."

A babble of voices surrounded him.

"What did the kid say?"

"That's crazy!"

"Forget it – no way was anyone shot!"

Zak didn't argue. He'd be proved right when the police arrived and did their forensics.

He stared across the road. The back end of the bus was full of leaping flames. Ugly black smoke billowed up. The kids were on the other side of the road, huddled together, crying, terrified, being comforted by adults.

Someone ran towards the bus. "We have to get Chet!"

"He's dead!" Zak yelled. But the man ignored him.

A voice called out urgently. "Keep back – the gas tank could blow!"

The man hesitated, already halfway across the road. He was still standing there when a fierce explosion rocked the bus and a plume of oily black and red fire rolled up into the sky. The man turned and ran, his arms up to cover his head. A couple of metres closer and he'd have gone up with the bus.

Zak reeled back from the searing heat.

If he hadn't stayed and checked, the kid would be dead. He wiped his sleeve over his dirty, sweating face. The boy he'd saved was standing close by, conscious now and shaking. It was Brandon Fine.